HEALING HEARTS

HEARTS OF HIDDEN HILLS

SUSAN LOWER

TIME GLIDER BOOKS

DEDICATION

Those who are planted in the house of the LORD
Shall flourish in the courts of our God.

HEALING HEARTS

1

Violet Harding stood near the window of the church social hall. Swirls of dusty white snow danced across the parking lot outside. She wrung her hands.

Behind her, the basement vibrated with chatter as the ladies of Hidden Hills filled their plates with finger sandwiches, mini cheesecakes, and pretzels. Pink and blue streamers twisted across the tables and hung from the ceiling.

Her mother approached. "Here, you need to eat."

Violet glanced down at the plate of food, shoved it away, her appetite rebelled against the combined smells of tuna fish and cherries. She stared back out the window, counting the snowflakes that touched the window pane. The weatherman forecasted another two or four inches of snow by later in the evening. She should have stayed home where it was warm and comfortable.

"You're way too thin," her mother said. Violet turned away from the window and her mother to gaze out across the social hall. She spotted Anne who owned the beauty salon in town a few tables over. She debated going to say hello, but decided she would see her in a few days when she made her delivery of handmade shampoos and lotions to Anne's shop.

Elaine clucked her tongue and set the plate down on a nearby table, drawing Violet's attention back to her mother. "Don't, Violet. Don't ruin this day for all of us."

That was easy for her mother to say. Violet kept her eyes fixed on a particular woman standing amongst a group of ladies. If not for the pestering of her mother, Violet would have preferred to stay home. It wasn't like anyone would have noticed her absence, except for Elaine.

"You know what today is," Violet whispered, more upset with herself than her mother. She shouldn't have let Elaine guilt trip her into attending. Today was not Gloria's, nor Violet's brother Nathan's, nor even her mother's day. Oh no, this day had been reserved long ago. It belonged to her... and Kyle.

But she honed her gaze on Gloria, her brother's pregnant wife, and tried to keep the swirling emotions inside her at bay. She tried to be happy. She *wanted* to be happy. Why had God taken it away?

Gazing at her sister-in-law, Violet's lungs felt heavy as if they couldn't take in any more air. She shook her head, trying to clear away the memory of today's date.

Gloria's pink dress stretched across her belly and did nothing for her bland complexion. Her frizzed hair was pulled back in a large clip, and Violet would have liked to cut it short.

"Honey," her mother said, giving Violet's arm a light squeeze. "You can't keep blaming him."

She could, and she would.

She'd lost everything, and her brother had it all. Her hopes. Her dreams. The future that should have been hers. Nathan and Gloria were living their happily ever after while she continued to grieve the loss of her own.

A wave of sorrow swelled inside her like a tidal wave rising in the ocean. She closed her eyes, waiting for the feeling to pass. She never felt so lonely in all of her life.

Two years ago, she'd stood in this hall surrounded by

women, gifts, and well wishes. But not for a baby like Gloria and Nathan. No, for the wedding that would no longer come.

For a moment, she was swept back to another time in this hall, one far better than the present.

Violet covered her burning cheeks with her hands. On her lap lay an opened garment box. Lingerie nestled in layers of tissue paper.

"You wear that on your wedding night," one of the ladies called out.

"Don't let him see it before then," another voice laughed.

"Lord, they'll never make it to the church if he does."

Grief slammed into her chest, knocking her back to the present.

She gulped for air.

"Are you all right?" Elaine touched her arm.

Slowly, Violet opened her eyes, knowing that soon another reminder of the life she'd lost and her brother had gained would be forced upon her.

"Violet?" Her mother leaned closer, her eyes widened with alarm.

"Go away." Her voice trembled.

Her mother sniffed a quick breath and pulled back her shoulders.

"Elaine," Gloria called, beckoning Violet's mother to the other side of the hall.

Elaine looked from Gloria to Violet, clearly torn. Then, with a reluctant sigh, Elaine walked in Gloria's direction.

"I think you may have hurt her feelings." A rich, resonant voice startled her from behind.

Violet spun around. "Who?"

A pair of soft brown eyes stared down at her, as an unfamiliar man pushed his sunglasses into thick curls of unruly sandy brown hair. Lifting a suit-coated sleeve, he pointed toward Elaine's retreating figure. "Your mother."

"How do you know she's my mother?" Violet asked, willing her pounding pulse to steady. Her gaze drifted down over his trim frame. What was he doing here?

Didn't he know this was a women's party?

And more importantly, how did he know her mother?

He looked as if he'd just stepped off a beach rather than come in from a snowstorm. She doubted he'd find any sand, let alone a beach, here in Kentucky. Besides, what kind of man wore sunglasses in November?

"You look like her. Unless I'm mistaken and she's your sister." He winked.

Violet's chin notched a degree higher as his curious eyes assessed her. "I don't have a sister."

"I assumed Gloria …"

"Is Nathan's wife," Violet said, uncertain how he knew so much about her family.

"Nathan being your brother, right?"

Violet opened her mouth and then clamped it shut. It was better to say nothing at all to this man than to say something she'd regret later. Why couldn't people leave her alone?

"Hey, it looks like I came just in time." He nodded towards women gathering in the center of the hall.

With Elaine on one side of her and a plump woman on the other, Gloria sat with an unopened gift in her lap. Violet's mother curled a finger, smiling and beckoning her daughter to come and sit amongst the other women. Ignoring her, Violet turned back to the tall stranger. "If you're looking for the sportsmen's club, it's down the street."

Bleached white teeth peeked out from his grin. "Thanks, I'll remember that."

No man she knew attended these girly functions—except Kyle. An image of his handsome face came to mind, and her stomach fluttered.

The room started to turn, and she reached out, gripping the stranger's coat sleeve.

"Hey," he said, his tone soft. "You okay?"

Violet wanted to nod her head, confirm she was, but that would have been a lie. She would never be *okay* again.

His warm hand closed over hers, and his brown eyes gazed down at her. She blinked, not wanting to read beyond the surface of his gaze. He had the same expression she saw all too often. Pity.

Pulling her hand away, Violet tore her gaze from him. Those eyes probed deep into a place where she'd never allowed anyone to enter. Not ever again.

She didn't want his pity. Poor Violet this, and poor Violet that. She'd had enough pity to last a lifetime.

She backed away. "I ... I have to go."

He held her by the arm. "Wait ..."

"If you know what's good for you, you'll leave this place, too." She tried to shake him off, decided to take another step back, but he held on. She stared at his fingers then his face, silently pleading for release.

"Meaning?"

Her gaze darted around the hall. Gloria sat opening gifts, while ladies sampled from their plates and sipped Hawaiian Punch. Chatter, laughter, and emotional responses came from Gloria's audience.

Violet felt the heat radiate from his touch past her elbow. She flushed. Taking a deep breath, she tried to politely regain ownership of her arm.

"There you are." An elderly woman waved at them.

Violet recognized the woman as her rouged lips, and purple eye shadow came into clearer view. Mrs. Jones. The woman never paid full price for anything, including the cosmetics Violet sold.

"You're early," Mrs. Jones held a frail hand out to the stranger.

If Violet were to escape, it had to be now. Otherwise, she feared she'd be trapped talking shop with Mrs. Jones and lured by Elaine to join the festivities. Mrs. Jones was hobbling near. Violet peered over at her mother, whose head was bent in conversation.

Stumbling back on her two-inch heels, Violet slipped from the stranger's grasp and retreated. As he reached for her, he called out her name, "Ms. Harding!" But she pushed through the double doors like a woman being pursued.

From the other side of the doors, high-pitched laughter mocked her.

"Take care of this for me, will ya?"

Seth Jones peered up from scanning the classified ads in the local paper. His attention, however, had been fixed on a certain cheeky female he'd encountered at a particular baby shower.

His gaze lifted to his partner, Tracy Smith. She walked in, juggling a stack of files and holding out a folder in his direction.

"New client?" he asked, reaching for the folder.

"In a matter of speaking," Tracy said, dumping her load on the chair behind her. Folders and papers sat stacked neatly on either side of him and against the walls, without a filing cabinet in sight.

Three months ago, he'd downsized to a smaller office, sold off some of the furniture, and let go of all but himself and Tracy. They formed a partnership after Seth struggled to as a broker to keep his real estate business afloat in Shelbyville. Too much competition and not enough houses persuaded him to move. That, and his grandmother needed him more often in her old age. Opening up a place in Hidden Hills made more sense and gave them the advantage of traveling between the other smaller towns in the area. It wasn't the big business he once envisioned, but he believed in God's promise of provisions.

Now Tracy maintained her own clients, answered phones, and handled the rental properties, while Seth took care of keeping them out of the red. Sometimes he wondered if her faith in him was a little misplaced. She should have gone with the others to seek new listings and a new broker to prosper elsewhere, but Tracy assured him she and her family could manage through the transition. He prayed things would pick up for them when spring came. People moved away. Not many came here to stay.

"It's pretty cut and dried by the looks of it." Tracy laid the folder on his desk from her stack.

"Then why are you handing it off to me?" Seth sat back, folding his arms across his chest.

"We got another rental I need to list over by the lake, and if I get time, I thought I'd try to bring these stacks down a little." She waved her hand at the mess behind her. "Unless you'd like to take up filing …"

"Ready to put the sign up?" Seth asked. It wasn't like Tracy to pass up a chance at the extra commission. Although, he couldn't blame her, rentals at the lake provided more of a steady income on commission than house sales these days.

"Spoke to the lawyer myself, faxed in the contract a little bit ago. The place is ready to go on the market today." She cleared off some papers and found a seat on the other end of the desk.

Seth flipped through the folder, briefly glancing at the contract.

"That is if you can get all parties to agree." Tracy's large gold hoop earrings jiggled by her neck as she flipped her long strands of raven hair back.

Seth whistled low under his breath. "There's a lot of red tape here, I'm not sure it's worth getting involved."

"That's fine if you don't want it. I'll take it. The Freeman's are friends of my Uncle Cliff, that's why they offered the contract to sell to us. I understand if you don't want it. I hear working with Violet Harding can be a *joyful* experience."

At the mention of Violet Harding's name, he envisioned

her. He wasn't sure 'joyful' was the right way to describe her. Wheat-ripened hair flowed down around her shoulders, and those eyes had haunted him since the day he'd first run into her at the church social hall. Something about her made his stomach churn, or perhaps it was his chest. No matter what it was, his dormant heart had stirred.

She certainly came with a lot of red tape. Especially for him. It had become his experience in this line of work, that where lawyers were involved, it plainly spelled divorce.

His gut twisted.

"What do you know about her?"

Tracy shrugged. "Just gossip. Her family owns a place over by Shelby Lake. I guess it belongs to her brother now. Your grandmother would know more since she was invited to the baby shower."

"You could have went," Seth pointed out.

"Women having babies is contagious and I've got enough that I don't need another one. I'm new around here, remember? You're the one who moved us to this place to save on overhead."

He did, and he was grateful for Tracy keeping up with their rental properties, especially around the lake. So far, they had proven the best income stream.

"The best way to get to know people is to join in community activities. Isn't that what you told me?" Seth grinned.

"Which is why I suggest you visit your grandmother more often. If anyone knows about anyone, your grandmother or her friends will give you the low down," Tracy said with a huff. "Don't get me wrong. I feel bad about her situation, but business is business."

Had it been him, or was it all men that caused the walls of defense to rise in Violet Harding? A divorce would undoubtedly explain her reaction, but there was something more, something profound and vulnerable he'd witnessed the day of Gloria and Nathan Harding's baby shower. He pressed his lips together, refusing to ask Tracy to spill gossip she may have heard. He wanted to get to know Violet without any preconceived assumptions.

"Well?" Tracy hopped off the desk.

"A client is a client." His response went against his first inclination to avoid deals like this one. But the commission tempted him. What he'd seen in Violet Harding's eyes, however, tugged at a place inside him he hadn't opened in years. Something about the way she'd looked at him, desperate, pleading, and grieving. Then her hostility, a defense mechanism he was sure, for he had found himself being less than hospitable a time or two.

He didn't know how to help her deal with the heartache, but he could help her move on by selling this house.

2

With one eye open, Violet peered at the double-ringer alarm clock. The small hand hung on seven, and the long hand pointed to the three. As time passed, neither hand moved.

When was the last time she'd remembered to wind her clock?

She rubbed her eyes with the heels of her hands.

She eased off the covers, fumbled for her robe, and slipped it on as she walked out of her room. The aroma of fresh-brewed coffee drifted down the hall, teasing her nostrils. Violet headed downstairs toward the kitchen, lured by the coffee and scents of baked blueberries. She padded, barefoot, across the cool ceramic floor as she knotted the belt of her terry cloth robe, and stifled a yawn.

"Good morning," her mother said, pulling mugs out of the cupboard.

Violet blinked, disoriented from her morning doze.

"Have a seat. The muffins will be cool in a moment."

"What are you doing here, Elaine?"

"I seem to recollect a time when you used to call me 'Mother.'"

Violet eyed the older version of herself. Her mother

reached sixty last month, but the flaws of age had barely touched her timeless skin. Violet saw to that, supplying her mother with creams and lotions she made with her own hands.

Elaine turned her back on Violet, as she popped muffins from a hot tin and onto a clean plate. She hummed and smiled over her shoulder.

"What are you doing here?" Violet edged around the counter and took a seat at the small breakfast nook.

"What does it look like I'm doing?" Elaine turned, placed a dish of butter and a plate of muffins down on the table between them, and said, "Really, Violet, it's almost ten o'clock! I called twice this morning."

Violet picked up a muffin and broke it in half. "I was sleeping."

These were the mornings she regretted giving her mother a key to her house. One day she'd rectify that mistake. This morning, however, the muffins smelled too good.

"I suppose I should be glad it was ten o'clock this morning, other days its noon before you rise, and don't you dare deny it." Elaine pointed out, as she poured them each a cup of coffee at the counter.

"Shouldn't you be sitting at work or over at Nathan's place helping Gloria sort through all the baby stuff." Violet's heart squeezed thinking of yesterday. Her therapist told her many times to identify the emotion, acknowledge the emotion, and move on. How long before the grief settled to a place where it didn't feel like it would swallow her whole?

Elaine raised a brow. Her mother worked in the borough office as a secretary. This morning, her mother lacked the usual pleated slacks and tailored blouse. She wore a sweater over a pair of leggings.

"You didn't answer my question." Violet said, stuffing her mouth with another piece of muffin. Working for herself had it's perks. She was a grown woman, and her own boss. What did it matter to anyone if she decided to sleep in?

"I did." Elaine placed a steaming cup of coffee under Violet's nose. She added two teaspoons of sugar and a dollop of milk before Violet began to stir. "I made muffins."

She took a seat opposite of Violet. "Now, I'm having brunch with my daughter. After all, it can hardly be called breakfast, could it?"

"Are you done lecturing me now, or should I wait to eat my muffin?"

Elaine sighed, put sugar in her own coffee, and stirred, not saying a word as Violet finished her muffin and grabbed a second. From the end of the table, Elaine slid a paper in Violet's direction. "I found this while I was baking."

Violet paused, looked down at the letter from the lawyer who represented Kyle's family in Sparta. This wasn't the first letter she'd received, and like all the rest, she chose to ignore it. Kyle put her name on the title when his aunt Joan passed the summer before their wedding date.

"How long have you known?" her mother asked.

Violet slathered butter on her muffin. "It's not important. Empty threats, that's all it is." Kyle's family wouldn't give up until they took everything Kyle left behind. She lost the love of her life. They lost a son. Nothing could ever replace them. Why couldn't they respect his wishes and move on?

Her mother's eyes grew nearly as large as the mouths of their coffee cups, staring at Violet. Elaine's jaw hung, but she managed to speak, "You can't live your entire life acting as if nothing happened. You can't ignore this." Elaine picked up the letter and shook it in Violet's face. "They're selling *this* house."

"It's threats."

"No, my dear child it isn't. According to the letter you failed to appear in court and a judge has awarded the Free-man's the house."

Violet choked. Her muffin caught in her throat. *This house?* They were going to sell *her* house? "No. They can't. It's in my name."

"Did you know there was a court date?"

She shook her head as if that would make it all go away. Since Kyle's death, his family had been trying to force her hand. And here she was, the day after the anniversary of his death, losing him all over again.

She and Kyle had planned to raise a family in this house, and live in it until they were too old to care for themselves. His family couldn't sell this house. Who did they think they were, trying to take away *his* house from her? *Their home.*

"They can't sell this house. My name is on the deed," she stated firmly. A judge couldn't take away someone else's property and give it to someone else, could they?

"But so is Kyle's." Elaine reached out and placed her hand over Violet's on the coffee cup. "Did you at least call our family lawyer?"

"That Hayes guy?" Why would she pay someone hundreds of dollars an hour to read a letter when her name was on the dead. It was cut and dry.

"Francis, dear." Since when was her mother on a first name basis with an attorney? "He took over when his father retired last year. Arthur and Lillian moved down to Florida last winter."

She loved how her mother knew everything about everyone in this small town. For the past two years, she tried hard to keep to herself. The first few months of Kyles death people came to the house with food. Then they offered to help her pack Kyle's things. The boxes still sat unpacked in the guest room across from the master bedroom. Kyle put his stuff there a few days before the accident. He insisted she get settled first. It never felt right to open the boxes or ship them off to a donation center.

"You knew you couldn't live here forever."

Had she? She picked up the letter and scanned the lines. Thanks to Kyle's family and a court ruling, she was left with little choice in the matter.

When she'd received the first letter, she'd offered to pay Kyle's family half the value of the house, but they wanted more. They asked too much of her, and so this, she deemed, had been as her mother implied, "only a matter of time." It was more of an ultimatum coming from them, and she refused to back down.

"I'll appeal. I can say I wasn't ever notified of the court date."

"Did you sign for any of the letters?"

Of course, and she just tossed it aside along with the others. Violet looked at the ceiling and closed her eyes for a long moment. *What else will you take away from me?*

When Violet was young, her mother told her that what God gave he could take away, but He'd never place more burdens on her shoulders than she could bear. Right now, she wasn't sure she could manage to stand, let alone handle one more loss.

Elaine pointed to the letter. "They're using Smith and Jones Realty, I believe that's Mrs. Jones' grandson."

Humming a tune under his breath, Seth slung a sign over his shoulder and walked down the sidewalk toward the colonial two-story home in Hatton, a town twenty minutes east of Hidden Hills. The house sat wedged between two other similar style houses on the street. It's exterior brick style mimicked all the other homes in this neighborhood. The porch was carpeted, and a black rail ran along each side. Bushes grew up against the porch posts, but they hadn't been maintained, he noticed, in quite some time.

Seth set the sign into a bare spot in the front lawn and

pulled a hammer out from his pocket. The northern winds blew strong across the landscape. He pulled the collar of his black wool coat up around his chin and pounded the wooden sign into the frozen earth.

A car drove down the street. He heard a door slam and muffled voices from a television coming from the house next door.

"You!" Violet came rushing off the front porch like a storm cloud gathering momentum. "Stop! What do you think you're doing?"

Seth paused long enough to look up and see Violet running towards him. Her hair billowed out behind her in the wind. But he couldn't allow himself to become distracted. He'd come here with a job to do. "Afternoon."

He swung his hammer down on the signpost again.

"Stop!" She grabbed the hammer.

Seth sidestepped her, and when she grasped hold of the handle, he swung her hand along with his down on the sign. She struggled to wrench the hammer from his grasp. "Give it to me!"

Seth jerked the hammer back. Violet held on, refusing to let go.

"It's good to see you again." He said, tugging the hammer back towards him.

Violet yanked the hammer back in her direction. Steam pouring from her nose and mouth like a dragon's breath on this cold afternoon. "Let go!"

"Not on your life." He clenched his fingers around the handle. His knuckles turned white.

"You can't do this." He heard the desperation in her voice.

"I've got papers saying I can," he assured her.

Violet lifted her chin, looking down her nose. Her gaze fell to their grips on the hammer. Seth tightened his hold on the sign. Afraid any moment, it would teeter, like his resolve. Her pleading expression stabbed him in the heart.

Her lips twitched, half smiling at him. Seth loosened his hold on the sign. She widened her stance. Using her free hand, she shoved on the sign. It toppled over and fell into a patch of snow. "Oops."

From the first moment he'd met Violet Harding, he knew she'd be trouble. He'd felt it deep in his bones. So why had he gone looking for it?

"That wasn't very nice," he said, slowly, deliberately, pulling the hammer back towards him. If she thought he was going to let go, she was mistaken. Instead, he matched her stance and prepared for a stand-off. His eyes lowered and caught sight of her bright pink socks.

At this rate, it wouldn't take long. Praising God that Violet had been in such a flurry to dissuade him that she'd forgotten to put on shoes. She wouldn't last much longer, standing on the frozen ground in twenty-degree weather.

"Who says I'm nice?" she asked, with a determined glint in her eye.

"You're going to catch your death standing out here without a jacket or shoes." If the chill hadn't set into her cable knit sweater already.

"As if you care about my health." She glowered at him. "Just let go and get off my property!"

"I can't do that," he snapped, irritated at the sudden odd mix of emotions that swirled inside him. He sucked cold air into his lungs. Pain spread through his chest, suddenly mirroring the desperate hopelessness he saw in this woman's eyes.

She sensed his moment of uncertainty and pulled back hard on the hammer. Seth didn't relent. He gripped the hammer with both hands.

Violet took hold of the hammer with the other hand. Her hands locked around his, she glared at him. "This is just a big misunderstanding."

"Then why don't we go inside, and you can explain it to me. Right after I finish putting up the sign."

Her eyes riveted to his face.

There had to be an easier way than this to make a living. Even though he'd drawn his own conclusions, it wasn't in his business to find out why. His company had been appointed to sell this house by the Freeman family attorney, and that's what he would do.

"Fine." A tremor ran up through her body, and she shifted her stance. At the same time, when he thought she would pull, she pushed the hammer towards him, and the blunt end of the hammer smacked him in the nose. Seth dropped the hammer and clasped his hands over his face, howling.

His vision blurred. Pain shot up his nose, across the bridge, and darted into his head. He stumbled back and fell to his knees. Her horrific expression as the hammer hit him flashed in his subconscious. He bent over.

Violet crouched beside him. "Are you okay?"

"I think you broke it," he mumbled, doubling over.

He rocked back and forth, blood seeping through his fingers. Violet took him by the arm and pulled him up. Seth wavered. He squinted at her.

She wrapped her arm around him and guided him inside the house.

Dragging him into the kitchen, she pulled out a chair and sat him down. She yanked open every drawer, muttering to herself.

He listened as she ran water in the sink. A moment later, he felt the cold, wet cloth pressing into his hands.

"Thanks," Seth choked, tilting his head back and covering his face with the cloth.

"Do you really think it's broken? I ... I c-can call an ambulance. Or ... d-drive you to the h-hospital if you w-want."

Seth grunted in response. Pain throbbed across his face,

and his head pounded worse than any hangover he'd ever experienced. He moaned.

"I'll get you some ice."

From behind him, he heard her exhale a shuddering breath, and the freezer door closed. He craned his neck, but the movement caused more pain to shoot down through his nose.

"Here, let me take a look at that," she held an ice pack in one hand and shooed his hands away with the other.

Without taking her gaze from his, she brushed away his hands and gently placed the ice and cloth on his nose. Her gentle expression touched him.

"The ice will help stop the bleeding." Her hands trembled. When his gloved hands slid over hers, she pulled away and stepped back.

Seth winced, holding the cold pack to his face.

Taking a deep unsteady breath, she said, "I'm sorry. I shouldn't have let go like that. I don't know what came over me. Sometimes I act without thinking."

Blood drained from his face leaving his cheeks cold and his flesh suddenly clammy. He took deep breaths through his mouth as he fought against the waves of nausea.

"I think … I'll take … that trip … to the hospital … now," he said between gulps for air.

Violet's pulse was racing.

Surely, from the adrenaline rush of the incident, rather than the thrill she'd experienced looking into his eyes.

She stopped her pacing, lowered herself into a chair, deeply humiliated, and irritated that she'd given way to one of her failings—a tendency to lash out when she felt herself being threatened.

And Seth Jones most certainly classified as a threat, in more ways than one.

She buried her face in her hands. The quiet of the ER ward sent every nerve in her body alert. Smells of antiseptic and new carpet sent shockwaves of sorrow through every cell of her body. She should go home, brew a cup of tea, or even go visit her mother.

Or maybe she could try that new recipe for a facial scrub. Anything, but this mindless waiting.

Outside, the sounds of sirens jolted her. Suddenly chilled, she pulled her jacket more tightly around herself and curled up on the metal-framed chair. Across from her, she noticed a woman and a child sitting huddled together with their heads bent as if they were praying. What good would prayer do now?

She'd broken his nose, hadn't she?

How many times had she run to the freezer to cure a bloody nose, a scraped knuckle, or ease a sore spot for Kyle? She swallowed the lump in her throat.

Besides, God knew her thoughts, didn't he?

Part of her wrestled with coming here at all. She could have dropped him off and been on her way, but those dark eyes had caused her stomach to quiver. From within the depths of Seth's eyes, she recognized uncertainty.

She tucked her cold hands in her jacket pockets as the sliding glass doors opened. A rush of chilly air brushed across her cheek.

A raven-haired woman lowered her hood and unwound her scarf. Violet watched as she approached the registration desk. As she leaned forward on the counter, her gold hoop earring glinted under the low lights. Violet strained to hear their conversation, but the woman's words fell short of her ears. Mariah, the nurse who assisted Seth back the hall earlier, appeared to speak to the other woman near the reception desk.

Mariah pointed, and too ashamed by her actions, Violet looked away. She sat, listening to the sharp clicks of the other woman's heels echo down the hall.

She should have looked for a wedding ring on his hand. Not that it mattered. A man like Seth wouldn't ever be interested in her. No did she want him to be. The past several hours became a blur in her mind. Violet brought her knees up and hugged them to her body. From the other side of the counter, she heard someone typing on a keyboard and someone shuffling papers.

Another cold breeze swept up her back, and she shivered.

She waited, waited for the congestion in her chest to clear, for the all too familiar sounds to go away, and for the doctor to walk out from around the corner.

Here, she remembered the last time she'd sat in a waiting room, in a chair, just like this. Only in a different hospital. She'd felt cold then, too.Guilt of Seth's injured nose kept her planted in the ER waiting room instead of going back home as soon as she handed him off.

A male nurse, wearing dark blue scrubs, walked down the hall in her direction. Violet let go of her knees and sat up. He shot a sympathetic look in her direction. Her heart pounded.

Then, the male nurse veered right and walked past her to the woman and child. He crouched down as the woman leaned forward, her blonde hair flayed out. The child, not more than a few years old, snuggled closer to his mother. Violet caught a glimpse of a white-coated doctor walking up to join them.

Her heart seized.

Slowly, Violet lifted her eyes to the face of the white-coated doctor. She blinked back the sight, right behind her eyes, of another doctor standing in front of her, looking sympathetic as he gave her the same bad news, as she suspected the woman and the child were receiving, right now.

The doctor extended his arm, and the woman stood up

and lifted the little boy in her arms. Violet's breath caught in her throat. As the woman walked past her, Violet noticed the woman's skin tone had paled. The little boy buried his face in his mother's neck, and she, too, wanted to cry.

Violet looked away, her throat closing with a rush of emotions. Hating herself for the fact she couldn't leave. What if that woman was here for someone else?

As they disappeared down the hall, Violet heard the tapping of the keyboard resume. She stood, pacing the empty area. In her pocket, Violet felt the weight of her cell phone. She yearned to call her mother. A tiny voice in her head repeated the phone number. She pulled out her phone and started to dial. Midway, she halted. She leaned against the wall, pressing her forehead to the cool paint. With few friends, having closed herself away from the world when she lost Kyle, her mother was the only and last person she had to call.

From down the hall, she heard the sharp clack of heels on the floor and a squeaky wheel. Slowly, she turned her head as Seth came into view. Immediately, Violet rose. Mariah, in her purple scrubs, pushed Seth in a wheelchair down the hall towards the exit with the raven-haired woman strutting down the hall beside him.

The woman stopped and turned. Violet braced for the confrontation. The woman's dark eyes swept over Violet. She wanted to cringe. Violet tilted her chin and stared back at the woman. Hard.

And then Seth looked at her. Violet must have jarred a few brain cells loose when she hit him. He slid the ice pack away from his swollen face and gave her a goofy grin. Her disobedient heart did a tiny jig.

The raven-haired woman scowled and pushed the ice pack upon his face, blocking Violet from his view.

She watched as the doors opened, and the nurse pushed Seth out into the hospital's parking lot, the raven-haired woman hot on his trail.

3

By Thursday, Violet was sure she'd seen the last of Seth Jones. Her kitchen windows were frosted. For several weeks, it seemed the residents of Hidden Hills were stuck in a cold front.

Today, however, there wasn't a flake of snow or a drop of rain in the forecast. It was a perfect day for running errands and delivering bottles of her handmade beauty products to the salons in nearby towns as the holiday season squeezed near. Already, several neighbors were taking advantage of the weather and stringing holiday lights. She packed boxes, preparing to load her car when she heard someone jiggling her doorknob.

She took a quick peek out the living room window before turning the deadbolt and yanking open the front door. Hunched over, fiddling with a key in one hand and attempting to keep his balance with the other, was the same man who'd gotten himself a broken nose the last time he'd been around her.

Seth Jones had been a nuisance from the first time she met him, she decided, leaning against the door jam and crossing her arms. She fixed her eyes on him. "It doesn't work." She jerked her chin toward the key in his hand when he stared up at her, surprised. "I had the locks changed weeks ago."

Slowly, he straightened. "Well, I guess that explains why I couldn't get in. I'm sorry if I startled you. Most people aren't home this time of day."

"Most people don't go around breaking into other people's houses," Violet said.

"It's good to see you again." He held out his hand. Dark circles hung around both his eyes like a raccoon, and a wide piece of tape ran across the bridge of his nose. It both annoyed her and humbled her to have him standing there.

She noted his height, a few inches above her own. She tilted her face up to study the man with the audacity to try to enter her home uninvited. She stood cross-armed blocking him entrance. His hand dropped.

She stared at him with the icy demeanor of a woman who knew the second she let herself fall into a man's arms, she'd put his life in danger. She couldn't allow that to happen, not ever again. Not that she'd think she could with a man like Seth Jones.

"I know all about you, Mr. Jones," Violet said. *Thanks to my mother.* She knew Seth Jones was an unattached thirty-some-thing man who, by her mother's recollection, had been attending the same church as her family for the past few years.

What she didn't know was why he was foolish enough to come back.

None of the others ever did. She'd gained a reputation after all the previous attempts by all the private investigators, legal associates, and friends of the Freeman family.

She'd sent them all packing. Word usually got around.

All she wanted was to be left alone.

"Well, then it would seem I am at a disadvantage Ms. Harding, as I barely know anything about you. Would it be too much for me to ask to come in? I promise to be on my best behavior." He touched his nose and winced.

He played the guilt card well, she decided, having no choice but to step back and motion for him to enter. She owed him that much.

Seth slipped off his jacket and walked around the room, briefcase in hand. "To be honest with you, I came here …"

"Just get on with it." Violet waved her hand as if she didn't have a care in the world. She appreciated his honesty. At the same time, she knew he hadn't come here for a social visit and was surprised to feel a pang of disappointment. "I hope they get a dollar for the place."

After all this time, resentment continued to pour from the wellspring of her heart. *This day I marry my best friend, but whose friend had Kyle been, hers or her brother's?* The three of them had been so intertwined throughout their youth that it had been hard to find where one friendship started and another ended. Perhaps that was why the puncture in her heart had been so slow to heal.

Seth sensed the change in Violet as if a black cloud hovered just above her head. And just like the day he'd met her at the baby shower, he couldn't shake this dissolute feeling. He touched her arm, and her shoulders slumped.

"I'm sorry you have to be going through this."

"I wouldn't have to be if you'd walk back through the door and forget you were ever here," she said.

"There are some things that you can't run from. Sooner or later, it catches up with you." He caught himself from reaching out to her. Not wanting to spook her and gain any more broken or misplaced body parts, he decided to treat her with caution. Remembering how she waited at the hospital for him, she unknowingly revealed a piece of herself he suspected not many got to see. With that knowledge, he also knew a woman with that much pain in her eyes had a right to wear an invisible shield. He did his homework, asked around. Okay, maybe just his grandmother, but it was a start.

Seth couldn't imagine a woman like Violet being easy to please, but he'd help her find a new home and pray that her heart would be open to letting go of this one.

He set down his briefcase on a nearby coffee table and shuffled through the papers stacked inside. His hands felt clammy and his nose throbbed reminding him of his last encounter, but he ignored it. Silently, Violet tilted her head to watch him.

She was a striking woman. Most women he knew draped themselves in designer clothes and wore painted beauty, but none of them compared to Violet. Her faded jeans and ribbed turtleneck complimented her frame—maybe his only criticism —she was too thin.

She wore her hair pulled back with a black band, and waves of rich honey curved around her face. A hint of pink graced her lips.

He held out a folder in her direction. "These papers contain all the information I was given."

"Why are you giving these to me?"

"Because this is your home and I assume no one shared these with you."

Violet took them from him. Her lips pressed thin. She sat on the end of a nearby sofa and read. From the grimace on her face, he guessed his assumption correct.

"Do you mind if I have a look around? Take a few pictures?" He sucked in his breath waiting for her response. If not him, his partner would take the commission, and deep down he felt he needed to handle this one. Cases like these were rare.

"What choice do I have?" She tossed the folder on the couch and motioned for him to follow her. Uncertain by her reaction, he hesitated.

"Change your mind?"

"No." He remembered the kitchen from his brief and painful previous visit there. At the far side of the kitchen was a door. "That leads to the basement where the laundry is located."

He gave her an empathic smile. They passed through the standard rooms of the dining room, living room, and she headed up the stairs.

"Two or three bedrooms?"

"Three." He heard the hollowness in her voice.

At the top of the stairs, he paused, took pictures with the camera from inside his pocket, and walked in and out of rooms. Violet leaned back against a wall, watching him beneath hooded eyes.

He lingered longest inside the master bedroom. If the bedspread hadn't been rumpled, it would have appeared that no one ever slept there. His gaze fell to the nightstand, where a Bible lay closed with a water ring staining the cover. He cleared his throat and backed out of the room.

Violet blushed and ducked her head as he stepped into the hallway. "Are any of the other rooms being used?"

"I live here alone, Mr. Jones, what do you think?"

She followed him back downstairs. She gathered his coat and handed him his briefcase. "I guess now that you've gotten what you've come for, you'll be going now."

Seth admired her willingness to concede to that which she couldn't change. Part of him wished he hadn't accepted that folder, but someone else would have come along in his place. An unfamiliar feeling struck him. If he didn't know better, he'd have thought he was jealous of the one who would take his position in Violet's life. What that exactly was, he didn't know.

"There's just one more thing." He braced himself. "I'll need a *working* key to the house and garage."

Violet arched a brow and planted her hands on her hips. "Whatever makes you think I'd give you the key to my home?"

"I understand your reluctance to cooperate, in the same position I would be, too, but if you allow me a key, I can place it in a box on the door and won't have to bother you when appointments are made to show the house."

She laid a finger alongside her cheek and tilted her head to one side. "So, if I give you a key, then I wouldn't have to be here during a showing of the house nor see you again? How would I know that you're just not going to pop up and come in when you feel like it?"

"I'll call you and arrange appointments in advance." He said, "And in the meantime if you would like, I can help you relocate to another home."

Her eyes gazed upon his face for a long second. Seth found himself holding his breath again. Violet turned on her heel, marching away, returning a few moments later with a key.

"House key?"

"There you have it," she said.

"And the garage?"

Her eyes narrowed. "Is off-limits."

"You understand …"

"No." She interrupted. "You understand. The garage is locked and off-limits until such a time as I say."

Seth recognized the sign of challenge in the hard stare of her eyes. Her spine stiffened, and his nose ached with a reminder of the last time he'd gone up against her. It made him wonder what she was keeping in the garage?

His grandmother had always taught him to choose his battles wisely. This was one battle he knew he would not come out the victor.

"But there will come a day," he said, taking the key from her hand.

"Not today," she said.

"I can appreciate you wanting the opportunity to pack

your things. Thank you for the key." He showed himself to the door. Behind him, he heard the deadbolt slide shut.

A few days later, Seth met a pair of newlyweds on the front porch of Violet's home. As he promised, he'd called and left a message. He'd arrived early, but so had his appointment.

The husband worked over in Hatton for a machine shop, and the wife commuted to a dental office not far from here. He recognized the excitement in the woman's eyes, and the let's-get-on-with-it attitude of the husband. This wasn't the first house he'd shown the couple in the weeks he'd been working with them.

"I think you'll like this place." He pulled the key out of the lockbox and inserted it into the knob. "It's only been on the market a few days."

"What about the neighborhood?" asked the man's wife, as they stepped over the threshold. Whatever Seth had on his tongue to say dissolved the moment he stepped inside behind them.

Gagging, the woman covered her face with her hands. The husband turned around and marched back out onto the porch. Seth held his breath, annoyed, and frankly, not surprised. Thanks to Violet and his broken nose, his sense of smell was diminished.

He ushered the woman back outside. "If you'll excuse me one moment, I'll see if I can find the cause of this.

"I'm not going back in there." The woman huddled close to her husband. "It smells like something died in there." She covered her mouth again, gagging.

"Just give me a minute," Seth urged. "I assure you it didn't smell like this when I was here last." He looked at the man who shrugged and rushed into the house, breath held, and searched for the culprit.

A dozen candles flicked their weary flames throughout the living room and dining room. They were almost at the end of their wick, much like Seth. He blew them out, one by one, none of them the same scent.

Long after the couple disappeared, he sat fuming. He'd left the front door wide open. When thoughts of going home arose, Violet walked in.

He'd rehearsed what he would say over and over again, but words failed him. Violet tossed her purse on a nearby chair and closed the door. "If you think you can freeze me out, you'll need to do better than that."

"I would think that you would want to thank me for letting in a little fresh air. One would hardly be able to breathe otherwise, but of course, you knew that, didn't you?"

Her eyes grew wide, and she planted a sweet smile on her face. He feared he wouldn't have enough patience to hold a civil conversation. He got up and walked past her, heading for the door.

"I heard candles were alluring to home buyers." Violet pulled off her gloves one finger at a time. "There are so many wonderful scents to choose from."

Seth closed his eyes for a brief moment. His nose ached. No man in his right mind would keep putting himself through this kind of torture—except Jesus. Seth sighed.

"You're only fooling yourself. You won't be able to scare off every buyer."

Violet blinked, her expression blank. "I don't know what you're talking about."

"No, I don't suppose you do."

~

Seth buried his hands in his hair. Violet Harding had turned out to be an impossible task. He'd never sell this house, let alone breach the defenses of her heart. Not that he wanted to, he dismissed the notion.

The woman was utterly and totally determined to undermine his efforts to sell her house. He reached for a folder and a stack of papers strewn across his desk. Beneath the pile, he spotted the corner of his Bible. For the second time that day, he pulled the little black leather book out from under the papers.

He'd been so focused on selling that house in order to add the commission to this month's sell's sheet, he hadn't stopped to think about the occupant inside it as anything more than a pest.

In truth, Violet Harding was a living, breathing, beautiful woman. He'd noticed it, a time or two, but forced himself to look the other way. Getting involved with a client wasn't part of his practice.

Besides, the last thing he needed on top of all the other problems in his life would be to get involved with a woman like Violet. Spiteful, unyielding, and she was as broken as they came. Broken, that made him snort, perhaps while picking up a few pieces of his own, he'd find himself lost in the puzzle that made up Violet Harding.

He touched his nose. He had that coming, taking a direct approach to all things had been his signature around this place. That kind of approach kept Smith & Jones Realty running afloat. Until now, when in recent months, they started floundering.

"It's your girl," Tracy called from the hallway. "Line two."

Seth settled himself in his chair and answered the phone, forcing his tone to remain neutral. "Ms. Harding, what can I do for you?"

"I've been thinking about what you said about needing a home, and I've decided I'd like to make an offer on the house."

Amused by her tactfulness, Seth sat up a little straighter in his chair. "You'd like to make an offer on the house you're currently living in?"

"The very one," her voice carried a bit of irritation across the line.

"Why don't you come into the office and we'll discuss your offer," he said.

"You are able to accept offers on the home, are you not?"

"I can certainly pass on your offer to the seller and notify you of their response." Seth hesitated and then dared to go on. "I'm not sure why you waited until now to make an offer when you could have worked this out with the attorney without a third-party interruption before the home was put on the market."

He heard her sigh, "I've already done that. They refuse to sell me the house. They don't want me living here."

"What makes you think they will accept now?" He tilted his head, listening for her response.

"Because you can present my offer to the other party without them having knowledge of the person who is making the offer, right?"

Seth had to give her credit. "Under normal circumstances, you would be correct."

He chewed on his lip, uncertain whether or not to reveal secured information. According to the instructions of the sale from the attorney, any offers from Ms. Harding were void. Rather than upset her, Seth responded, "What is your offer Ms. Harding and I'll pass it onto the sellers."

Violet stated her offer. "I would think it would be more than reasonable, seeing as half of the money from the sale will be coming back to me anyway."

Seth picked up a pen and scribbled large circles on a pad of paper. "I'll get back to you as soon as I hear from the other party."

He would call the attorney this afternoon as requested to give periodic updates on the sale. So far, he had several showings of the home that appeared less than promising due to Violet's ministrations around the house and one offer that was unacceptable by the seller's standards.

"You can call me when they counter. Good day, Mr. Jones." On the other end of the line, he heard the click.

4

Cold winds and a chance of accumulating snow couldn't convince Violet to stay off the roads and delay her trip around to all the strip malls in the neighboring town of Shelbyville.

She wouldn't sit around, waiting for Seth to call her back. She had places to go, people to see, and a business to run. Especially if the Freeman's decided to take her offer to the bank and sell her their share of the house.

They had no other choice. They had to accept Violet's offer. The Freeman's and Seth Jones would be out of her life forever, but the thought pressed heavily against her heart. She took a deep, cleansing breath of air to try to ease the discomfort.

The streets were filled with regular Monday traffic in Shelbyville. Outside the Cutt'n It Salon, things seemed quiet. She spotted the rental sign on the building a few storefronts down from where she'd parked. Suddenly, on impulse, she reached for a pen in her purse to write down the number, but it faded as quickly as it came when she spotted the Smith and Jones logo.

The photograph on the sign didn't do his handsome face justice. The vinyl print of his features couldn't capture those dark brown eyes or the crinkles at the side of his cheeks when he smiled.

Violet shook her head, the man showed up at every turn she made. Now, in her mind. Seth Jones presented a challenge to her heart.

Generally, most people wore a sorrowful accepting look when she came around. Her whole life had been wrapped around one man, Kyle Freeman.

From the first time she'd crashed her bicycle into him on the front lawn of her parent's house, she'd planned on marrying Kyle. She'd been seven, but age didn't matter. Kyle picked up her bicycle while her brother, Nathan, brushed her off. Even then, her eyes, like her heart, were locked on him. Now, however, her eyes always seemed to be fixed on a set of ominous brown ones.

Kyle was an adventurer, much like her wayward brother. A pair of daredevils, taking life to the fullest, their hearts bursting with faith and trust, and stupidity. She grinned. There were no mountains high enough, no rivers too long, or trails too narrow to discourage Nathan Harding from conquering them. Just like there wasn't a race track left in this part of the world that Kyle Freeman hadn't sped his car across.

She should never have allowed Kyle and Nathan to go off on one last adventure without her.

Violet slammed her car door shut, grateful for the gloves on her hands and the hat on her head. A few strands of her hair escaped and tickled the side of her cheek.

She took a quick glance at the window again of the empty storefront. From inside, two men emerged, one being Seth Jones.

Violet rushed behind her car, pulled up the trunk lid, and ducked her head. *Please, please, don't let him see me.* She made a fuss over selecting boxes and piling them atop each other to block the two men's views.

When she heard them talking close by, she peered out around the boxes. Seth shook hands with the man before he turned to leave, and he caught a view of her. He grinned and nodded towards her. "Ms. Harding, what a pleasant surprise."

She flushed, and warmth spread up her neck and spotted her cheeks.

"Mr. Jones." She pulled herself up to her full height and dredged up the best smile she could present on such short notice. "Fancy seeing you here." She eyed the boxes stacked and scoped out the door to the salon.

"I had an appointment." He hitched his thumb back behind him. "Here, let me help you with those."

"Oh, no, I can get them on my own." Violet struggled to lift the boxes and shut the trunk of her car.

"Are you sure?" Seth lifted a brow. "It's really no bother, and it looks like you've got a handful there."

"I've got it, really." She stressed, clenching her teeth as she wavered to balance the boxes stacked in her grasp. "Have you heard about the house?"

She rested her chin on the boxes. From his eyes, she saw that he had.

"I'm afraid they decided to decline." He stuffed his hands in his pockets. "I knew you were expecting a counter or an acceptance, but the sellers have stated flatly that any offer you make will be refused."

Her cheeks burned, and she chewed on her lip as the information stewed inside her. "Well then …" she didn't know exactly what to say, because, at the same time of her rising anger, a good douse of cold disappointment soaked her.

His eyes threw her off. Their tender expression startled her. She stumbled, taking a step towards the salon. He reached for her, and she jerked back. Boxes spewed across the parking lot.

Violet landed squarely on her bottom.

Seth crouched beside her. "Are you okay?"

"Fine." She blinked back, spikes of tears prickling her eyes.

Seth held out his hand. Ignoring him, Violet stood up. She brushed off her backside, feeling the cold snow trickle down her slacks.

At the same time, Seth and Violet reached to retrieve the fallen boxes. Their gazes locked. His face had changed from its dark purple bruised appearance to yellow and green at his nose. She marveled at the sunglasses holding back the herd of curls on his head.

Her face turned aflame, and she tore her gaze away.

"Here, let me help you?" He moved over to find one of the boxes that tumbled away from her.

"You may want to check inside to make sure nothing is damaged." He picked up a box and handed it to her before retrieving the others. "Here you go, are you sure I can't help you?"

Violet shook her head. She gritted her teeth and managed to respond, "Thank you."

Seth winked as he slid his sunglasses down over his eyes. "See ya around."

Outside Violet's front door, Seth heard the thrum of music that vibrated the panes of glass in the front windows. He knocked and rang the doorbell to no avail. Whatever Violet was doing inside, she wasn't answering her door.

She could be having a party, but with the window blinds down and not being able to recognize neighborhood cars from visiting cars parked on the street, he couldn't tell.

He used the key in the lockbox and let himself inside the house. Maybe he should have called first. He touched the cell phone at his hip.

He found no one in the entryway or the living room. He

called out her name and, "Is anyone home?" but lost his voice in the loud music.

Around the corner through the dining room, the potent smell hit him. He'd never expected to come across it in Violet's kitchen, but it made his mouth go dry like a man who'd been without a drink in ages.

He stepped inside the kitchen. Violet stood at the stove. He watched as she turned off the gas burner and reached for a measuring cup filled with a white substance. Her face flushed pink from the steam off the stove, and her voice rose to match the lyrics of a popular heavy metal Christian rock song. Seth took a deep breath and counted in his mind to ten, willing God to give him strength. He'd come too far in the past four years to give in now.

"It smells like a brewery in here," he shouted.

Violet spun around, the contents of her measuring cup scattered on the floor. Her other hand flew to her chest.

"I didn't mean to scare you," he shouted. "I knocked and rang the bell, but you probably didn't hear me over your loud music."

She squinted at him as she attempted to read his lips. She backed up, reached above the refrigerator, and hit a button on the stereo.

"Don't you ever knock? I have a doorbell, you know."

Seth chuckled and stuck his finger in his ear. "Sorry, as I was just trying to tell you, I did both, but doubted you could have heard me—or a thunderstorm for that matter—over the stereo."

"What are you doing here? Surely, you're not showing the house today, or you would have called." Violet turned back to the stove, scraping up small white shreds and sprinkling them into a boiling pot beside her. On the counter lined in a perfect row, were six cans of beer.

He leaned forward, seeing if they'd been opened, and

frowned. What had they taught him in AA? It had been so long since he'd felt he needed to go.

Violet took a spoon and stirred, first clockwise, then counterclockwise.

The aroma lured him. He stared at the cans, at Violet's hand stirring, and took a step closer, looking down at the boiling liquid. Amber bubbles rose and broke open.

"Are you showing the house?" Violet cleared the empty cans from the counter and tossed them in the recycling bin near the back door. "Because today isn't good for me."

"No," Seth took the wooden spoon she'd left in the pot and stirred the liquid. He lifted it, let the liquid drip slowly off the end, and fought the temptation to bring the brew to his lips. It smelled almost foul, and he pondered the ingredients.

"Unless you like tasting shampoo, I wouldn't do that if I were you." Violet reached out and took the spoon from him. Seth stepped back and cleared his throat, relieved, but at the same time, he felt the back of his neck burn.

"I don't have any more if that's what you're after." Violet cocked her hip and stirred the pot. "Beer has one purpose in this house: for making shampoo."

Seth cleared his throat again, searching for words. "That's a relief. For a minute, there, I was thinking that was really bad smelling soup."

Violet tilted her chin up, looked up at him with those penetrating violet eyes, and raised an eyebrow. "Next, you'll be telling me to bottle it up and sell it, right?"

"I suppose." He should just put his fist in his mouth and stop talking altogether.

"Well, I do. While I'm waiting for this to cool down, you tell me why you're here." She leaned back against the sink and crossed her arms.

"I thought perhaps you'd like to take the afternoon and look at a few houses with me."

"I can't. I have too much to do today. Besides, Elaine will be dropping by around supper to bug me."

"Elaine." Seth asked, "Your mother?"

"She comes over every few days, kind of like you're doing now." Violet shrugged. "It's not going to work."

Seth went over to the sink and inspected the bottles she had lined up across the countertop. Drooling over beer shampoo made his mouth go sour. He made a mental note to stop in at the next AA meeting, even though he'd been sober for nearly four years. The temptation to take a drink beckoned him, and some temptations weren't easily avoided, like Violet.

"What won't work?"

"You and Elaine, trying to get me to leave this house. You're like the Freemans, never happy unless you're causing pain."

He saw it then, the wash of pain through her eyes. Her delicate brow furrowed, and her lips turned down.

"This must be difficult for you. My own parents divorced when I was young. It wasn't pretty then, and I'm sure it's not any easier with or without children."

Violet paused, looked over her shoulder at him, and laughed, her high pitch broken by pain and amusement. "You think I'm divorced?"

She laughed again. "I'd have to have been married then, wouldn't I?" She turned back to the pot on the stove and stirred the cooling liquid. She kept her head ducked low to her task, but he saw how her shoulders slumped.

"I'm sorry. I assumed you were married. I had thought a few years ago …" He didn't get to finish his apology.

Violet turned. "You really don't know, do you?" Her voice lowered.

Seth shook his head.

Her eyes glazed with wetness. "Don't tell me you haven't heard the stories. You do go to the same church with your grandmother and Elaine, don't you?"

"I do."

"For a man who claims to go to the same church, you know so little. Surely, you can't expect me to believe you don't attend church and not listen to the latest gossip."

Old news by now, but it never struck her any less how the people treated her those few Sunday mornings when she would arrive, dragged by Elaine, for service.

"I don't pay much mind to gossip. It's particularly frowned upon by Jesus." Seth leaned back against the counter.

Violet reached past him for an empty bottle. "Oh, please." Violet rolled her eyes. "Spare me the gospel. I get enough of that from Elaine."

"Why do you call her Elaine?" Seth asked. "Why not, mother?"

Violet glanced out the kitchen window. Something deep in her eyes told him she'd gone to another place and another time. Her face took on a texture of worry, even pain. Blinking, she looked at him.

"You don't ever call your mother by her name?"

Violet stuck a funnel in the mouth of a bottle and ladled shampoo out of the pot.

"I don't remember." A trickle of sweat beaded at his brow. He tugged the collar of his wool coat. "She left when I was seven."

Violet paused. "It's hard when you lose someone."

What could he say to something like that? Men, obviously, had failed Violet in the past. *Lord, don't let me fail her now.* He didn't want to be added to her list.

She ladled more shampoo into the bottle.

Sensing her reserve, he changed the subject. "So, what do you say? Take a drive with me? We'll check out a few houses?"

She glared back at him.

Seth held up his hands. "No commitment. Just window shop, isn't that what you women like to call it?"

"I have everything I need right here." Violet capped the bottle.

"Really?" Seth shoved away from the counter. "You wouldn't like a bigger kitchen? Or a separate place to bottle your shampoo? Or concoct your other beauty elixirs?"

He knew it wasn't right using temptation to lure her away from this house, but he saw the dreamy expression on her face that she did and took it further. He spied a label on the counter.

"You could take Violaceae Beauty Products out of the kitchen and into a place of its own if you found the right place."

Her eyes glazed, looking at him like a kid sizing up a piece of candy.

She averted her gaze, capped a bottle of shampoo and turned towards him. "You're in for a tall order if you think you can find me a house that can make me give up the one I already have."

"I can try, can't I?" Seth grinned. "Why don't we take a look at the houses I've got lined up and then you can tell me what you like and don't like. Then I'll know what we're looking for."

He placed an empty shampoo bottle into her outstretched hand.

5

"Here we are." Seth stood back and allowed Violet to enter through the front door. An agent stood back in the far corner of the room. She smiled, spotting Violet and Seth walking inside the house.

Seth nodded at the woman, who smoothed down the wrinkles of her lime green pants. Dark streaks of rouge were painted on the woman's cheeks and lips. If it hadn't been for Seth's hand pressed into her back, Violet would have turned around and walked back outside.

Violet cringed. The woman wore so much make up that she could be mistaken for a clown. She imagined real estate agents jumping through hoops just to make a sale and sighed. She gazed around the house's interior. No matter how many houses Seth showed her none would compare to the one she lived in now.

Nothing about this place felt warm and inviting, not even the cocoa powder brown. She didn't need to see past the living room to know that she wasn't interested. The layout was all wrong. The location outside of Hidden Hills and closer to Shelbyville. Letting Seth take her to look at houses was a mistake. She figured she'd amuse him, not that a small part of her wanted to get to know him. He could be married for all she knew. And why would she care? She sighed, thinking this a waste of time for all parties involved.

"Please have a look around." The real estate agent's badge said, "Helen," and she invited them to tour the house. If not for Seth's hand touching her arm and a gentle tug, she would have turned around to leave. Instead, Violet followed Helen in silence. Seth trailed behind her. Violet glanced back several times as Helen led them from room to room.

Seth hadn't asked her for a price range, nor had he given her a price sheet for the house they walked through, but as they drove through the neighborhood, she felt she could do better than this, her current neighborhood carried more appeal to her.

"So, what do you think?" Helen asked as they reached the living room again.

Violet dug down into her small handbag and retrieved one of her business cards. "Call me." She handed Helen her card, "Not about the house. I make beauty products." Violet indicated the woman's lips that pursed out in a pout.

Helen stared down at the card, silent.

Seth escorted her out. "I take it you didn't like the house."

Violet wrinkled her nose.

"Do you always insult women before you try to sell them your products?" He opened the door for her to get into his vehicle.

"She looked like a circus clown without the suit," Violet said. But perhaps she'd come off being harsher than she had intended. Not that Violet could admit it to him, though. She reminded herself she didn't want to be here. She wasn't going to fall for his ploy, nor was she giving up hope, but neither did she insult people. Seth Jones had a way of bringing out the worst in her, or maybe it was the situation. No, she decided it was Seth and reminded herself to keep up the invisible shields she wore around him.

Seth slid inside the SUV beside her and started the engine. His eyes rolled up towards the ceiling.

"She'll call. You'll see." Violet crossed her arms. "So, where are you taking me now?"

"Home," he said.

Violet pulled her purse up on her lap. "Suit yourself."

Fifteen minutes later, Seth pulled up in front of another house. This one on the edge of town, still close enough for Elaine to come bake blueberry muffins. Violet leaned forward, assessed the length of the ranch home, and made a note of the U-shaped driveway. They weren't that far from where her mother lived, and for that, she crossed the place off from any possibility.

"I thought you said you were taking me home," she said, as Seth opened the door for her to get out.

"You never know, this could be your home." Seth gave her a sheepish grin. Violet sank her feet down into the thin layer of snow and waited for him to close the car door behind her.

"Shall we?" He held his arm out for her. Violet ignored him and strutted up the drive. Her rubber-soled boots slipped, and Seth caught her by the arm. "Careful, I wouldn't want you to slip and fall." He placed her hand in the crook of his arm.

Violet became quiet and looked away.

The house was vacant. It's wood floors bare and windows stripped of their treatments. She shivered. She couldn't imagine a fire in the empty hearth or the sounds of laughter from within the walls.

She paused in front of the master bedroom. How could she ever sleep in a place so cold ... so bleak ... so empty of memories?

This was Elaine's fault, and Nathan's. If they hadn't ...

She turned away from the bedroom. Pushed past Seth and headed down the stairs.

"Seen enough?" He followed behind.

"This place is too cold." She wrapped her jacket more firmly about her.

"Okay," Seth didn't argue, he led her back to his SUV.

"Please, just take me home." She leaned back into the seat, closed her eyes, and waited for him to start the engine. Her toes, like her heart, had grown numb.

"One more place, I think you'll like it."

Violet shook her head. "I've seen enough." She wanted to go home, crawl in her bed, and relive the memories of the house she called home. She wanted Kyle, his vibrant blue eyes, and his strength.

As she opened her eyes, Seth's expression changed. His eyes, brown unlike Kyle's blue ones, softened. A brown lock of hair hung over to one side, and she imagined him as a small boy. How adorable he must have looked.

She reached over and pushed back the lock of hair. Seth captured her hand in his, "Just one more house, Violet. Then I'll take you home."

"Promise?"

"As God is my witness."

Seth's fingers were coated by the fabric of his gloves. Sounds of cars whizzing past them filled her head. Her gaze met his. Inside, she no longer felt like she had control of her life. As if she were going around in circles, she held on to him.

"One more house," she said, her voice strained.

By the time they reached the next residence, Violet regained her composure and focused on the neighborhood. They weren't inside the town lines of Hidden Hills anymore. He'd taken her west, toward the more rural sections of Shelby County.

She didn't wait for him to open the door, but scooted out and walked around the front yard. A small building sat separate from the house, and to her delight, as she rubbed the dirt from the windows, she recognized the interior—a beauty shop.

"Can we go in here first?"

"Hold on a second while I get the key." Seth jogged through the snow to the front door of the house and grabbed the key out of the lockbox. Breathless, he came over to her and unlocked the door.

She flicked a nearby switch, but the lights remained off. She looked at Seth. He flicked the switch and said, "It's a fore-closure, the utilities have been shut off."

Inside her hope sprouted, she tried to resist it, but as she walked into the dim-lit beauty salon, she could imagine Violaceae's logo on the front of the building and customers parked in the driveway. She'd host parties, cut and style hair, and camouflage last-minute facial blemishes on brides.

A pang of sorrow tilted her view, and she walked back outside as a cold wind swept across her face and took her breath away.

"Ready for the house?" Seth ran his hand down her arm. She hugged herself and nodded.

Sunlight filtered through the windows. Violet walked into the kitchen and viewed the backyard from where she stood in front of the sink. Wide and as far as the eye could see, tall evergreens lined the back section of the yard. She could imagine children running and laughing. A swing set in the corner, the family, gathered on the patio, and sadness crept inside her heart.

This house couldn't be for her. This house was meant for a family with children and laughter.

Seth stood behind her. She opened the pantry door and glanced inside, then the laundry room, and found a bathroom. Its pine décor had long lost its scent, and the toilet lid was taped shut.

"You can never tell with a foreclosure what might be wrong. They're usually priced to sell because the banks want to get rid of them and recoup what they can quickly."

"The entire place is probably infested with problems," Violet said.

"People don't like to have their homes foreclosed, many of them are forced to move out, and some of them like to leave their mark before they go."

By that, he referred to the absent appliances or the hole punched in the wall near the door. Lucky for her, the toilet had been salvaged.

She sat upon it. At least at home, she didn't have to deal with all the headaches of maintenance and repairs. Kyle always took care of it, even when his Aunt Joan had lived there before them.

Seth leaned against the doorway. Kind and patient, unlike the stereotypical real estate agents she'd heard about, Seth waited.

"Nobody should be able to force you out of your home," she said softly.

"Unfortunately, many banks do."

"Or the lawyers of upset in-laws," Violet said. They hadn't been her in-laws, not really, even though they'd treated her like a daughter since the day Kyle had brought her home to meet them.

How quickly it all changed inside the lawyer's office one November afternoon. Kyle's family separated themselves from her, pushing her to a lone chair in the back of the room, while the lawyer read Kyle's last will and testament.

She'd never forget the looks on Robert and Miranda Freeman's faces when they discovered Kyle had deeded her half of the house and his car.

"I thought you weren't ever married."

She searched his eyes and found only confusion in them. "I'm not." She answered, "I haven't ever been, but almost …" Her voice faded. "Once."

"I'm sorry it didn't work out."

She heard those words too often in the past, followed by their pitied expressions and eyes full of sorrow.

"I wouldn't be here if it wasn't for them." She whispered. Hurt filled her. "They won't be happy until they've taken everything away from me." Slowly, her barrier of reserve crumbled. "As if it will all just bring him back like it were yesterday."

A wrenching sob tore out of her, one that not even she expected. It nearly doubled her over. She clamped her hand to her mouth and shook.

"Who?" Seth wrapped his arms around her. Without the will to resist, she leaned against him and tucked her head under his chin. His strong arms enveloping around her, like a warm blanket.

Her body shook with grief. As her anguished emotions expelled, something fresh and alive seeped into the hollowness of her heart.

Torn between wanting it and fearing it, she clutched his jacket, closed her eyes, and buried her tear-soaked face into his broad chest.

"Violet?"

Exhaling a shuddering breath, she said, "Kyle Freeman, my fiancé."

6

Seth leaned back, the name, Kyle Freeman was familiar. Digging deep into the recesses of his mind, he recalled a news report about the local race car driver who drowned in a boating accident.

Violet's eyes were rimmed with the moisture of tears. Her bottom lip trembled, and she captured it with her teeth.

"I had no idea."

Violet reached into her purse, pulled out a tissue, and dabbed her eyes. Their usual glint of green sparks was dulled by their watery glaze. Seth extended his hand to her, but she ignored it. With the composure of a royal princess, she rose before him.

She smelled like vanilla and coconut, fumes from her beer brewed shampoo, but sweet never the less. Seth would have complimented her on that sweet smell, but something told him she would only take it as an offense.

"You're the first," she tucked the wadded tissue back into her purse. She turned her head, checked her appearance in the mirror and frowned.

He wondered if every morning that she put on her

makeup if she thought she could cover what was buried inside her. What scars would he find under the mask she wore?

Seth glanced at his watch, "I think it's best if we go now."

"I just want to go home." Violet followed him into the kitchen. He pulled a card out from an inside pocket in his jacket and laid a card on the marble countertop. There were several other cards beside his and several more to come in the days and weeks of the house's listing.

She looked at the cards as they passed through the house and back out into the cold northern winds. As he opened her door, her shoulder bumped into his arm. He'd been so sure this house would be the one, and for a moment, he'd seen a spark of interest in her eyes.

Kyle Freeman, he shook his head as he walked to the other side of his SUV. Cold air blasted him in the face when he turned the key. Violet tilted her chin and stared out at the house. Her hands-on her lap, composed.

Even though the heat filtered inside the vehicle, Seth couldn't shake the cold seeping into his bones on the ride back to Oak Street.

As he pulled up in front of her house, he said, "I can appreciate your reasons for not wanting to sell this place."

She turned, her shoulder pressed into the seat, and her hand on the door lever. "So, you'll drop the contract and leave me alone then?"

Seth's hands held onto the steering wheel. He puckered air into his cheeks and blew out hard. "If not me, then they'll hire someone else."

"I have to admit, you almost had me fooled," she said, her voice grew low. "But you're still just like them."

"I'm sure they have their reasons," Seth said.

"They don't want me here." She sniffed. "They wanted the house to stay in the family, but since I wouldn't give it up, they believe neither party should have it."

"The Freeman family?"

"Kyle inherited this place from his aunt."

"Then added your name on as co-owner." Seth finished for her. This explained why she owned part of the house and not enough to stop the sale.

"Now, you understand why this place means so much to me."

"Hanging on to a place that was never really yours doesn't make sense," he told her, and then softened his tone. "Some people might say you're acting a little irrationally about it, not wanting the Freeman's to have back what was rightfully theirs."

Her eyes widened, and her powdered jaw dropped. She clutched her purse and jerked open the door. "For a moment, I thought you might actually be human. I was wrong. You're nothing but a low-down real estate agent out to make a buck selling my house."

"That's generally how I make a living." He realized too late the mistake he'd made as she slid out of his vehicle and slammed the door.

"Kyle Freeman?" Tracy exclaimed, "As in the race car driver?"

Seth nodded. He'd stayed up all night in prayer for Violet. He couldn't get her off his mind.

Violet Harding sobbing in his arms.

One moment she was strutting through a house, her demeanor cool as the outside breeze and the next, she was opening her heart and letting him inside her sorrow.

Her grief-stricken face tied him in knots.

Tracy leaned in, elbows on his desk. "Isn't he dead?"

"Almost two years." Since the day he'd taken her in the house when he held her, the hurt and pain in her eyes seemed to always haunt him.

Hurt and afraid, she'd insulted him.

He'd searched the internet for countless hours and found articles about the accident. Kyle Freeman hadn't died on any race track.

"And here you are ..." Tracy clucked her tongue. "This has got to be the worst case we've ever encountered."

Seth dug his hands through his hair. "I think I'm going to need a drink after this one."

Tracy sat back, her face sobered. "Now don't you start talking like that, God has brought you through worse troubles than this one."

"I'm praying you're right." It wasn't the house that bothered him as much as its occupant.

How could he sell Violet's house without losing what small thread of friendship strung between them?

"This came while you were out." Tracy handed him a stack of papers, opened bills that would have to wait for payment, and a sealed envelope addressed from a law office in Louisville.

"Anybody, we know?"

Seth opened the letter, scanned down through the contents, and felt a weight drop on his chest. "It looks like we're about to drop the price on the Oak Street property."

"Violet?"

Behind her, a printer hummed, and pages rolled out with Violaceae labels. "What is it, Elaine? I'm busy."

Violet heard the tension in the line. She squeezed her chin down and lifted her shoulder in effort to hold the cordless phone in place.

"I thought you'd like to know Gloria is on her way to the hospital."

"So ..." Violet reached for a batch of labels and cut them

one by one with a pair of scissors. She heard the chime, two o'clock, and she hadn't had breakfast yet. She supposed lunch would do since she'd slept in until noon.

"One of these days …," her mother said.

"I know. I'm going to wake up all alone."

"You'll wonder whatever happened to the people you love," her mother added.

Outside, the day appeared washed in gray, and a misty rain fell that pitted the snow and formed scabs of ice across the surface.

"He's dead, remember?" She snorted, "Oh, that's right, you've forgotten like everyone else that he ever existed."

"Nobody's forgotten; we've all moved on, just like the way Kyle would want us all to."

"You sound like his family. What next, my dress? Do you expect me to give that up too?" A bitter taste formed in her mouth. She laid down the scissors and headed for the kitchen.

"Someday, darling, you might need that dress. You never know what plans God has in store for you."

She didn't know why, but all at the same time, she wanted to scream, shout, cry, and claw at Elaine through the phone. Her voice came out thick and rough. "I believe *His* plans ended for me the day *He* took away Kyle."

Here she stood alone. What plans could God have for her now? What more could He take away that she hadn't already given Him?

Whatever Elaine said next became lost to her ears. She clicked the phone off, pulled the cord in the kitchen, and finished cutting her labels.

Just because her church attendance over the past few years was sporadic, didn't mean she'd forgotten God or her salvation. However, knowing God had let her dreams go unfilled and her heart to be broken caused her faith to waver.

Three dozen labels later and a half a dozen boxes of Violaceae's product, Violet stretched her arms and tilted her head. Outside her kitchen window, rain-streaked the glass. Winds howled, and the sky grew darker with the rumble of thunder heard from inside the house.

She hummed an old hymn. Her mother taught her to keep herself distracted from the sounds of Mother Nature's fury. Startled by a clap of thunder, she gripped the counter.

"It was only a thunderstorm," she told herself. The weatherman said it would turn from rain to ice by the next morning, but that didn't make her feel any better.

Another loud rumble of thunder nearly sent her to the floor. She'd never been able to overcome the tremors thunder evoked in her, even as a child. Nathan would always be there in the middle of the night, she'd crawl in bed with him, and he'd protect her from the scary sounds.

She slumped against the wall and slid down to the cool tiled floor beneath the window. "Grow up, Violet."

As the first round of tears spilled down her cheeks, she closed her eyes and sobbed. Nathan had always been so quick to come to her defense, protect her from harm, and where was he now? Where had he been when … She choked back the sobs.

She heard a loud bang, the thunder, and rain thrashing in the wind. She buried her face in her hands. She should've kept talking with Elaine, or at least until the storm blew over.

She listened to the winds howl and huddled closer to the wall.

"Violet?" a voice called out her name, and she looked up. "It's Seth, anyone home?"

She swiped at the tears and drew herself up, slowly, using the wall for support.

"In here," she called, pulling up the edge of her daisy print apron to wipe her face. Relief swept over her at the sight of him.

He stood inside the kitchen, dripping wet, and his hair

plastered to his head. "We've got to stop doing this ..." He paused mid-sentence and stared. "Hey, you okay?"

Violet nodded. Her knees felt weak and her legs a little wobbly, like she'd just swum a mile as she pushed away from the wall. "Just because you've got a lockbox on this place doesn't mean you can barge in on me whenever you want."

Seth slipped off his wet jacket and hung it on a nearby chair. "I've tried to call several times, but your phone seems to be off the hook. I was afraid it might have been because of the storm."

"I did that on purpose." She crossed her arms. Her pink blouse blotted at the sleeve with her tears. If Elaine couldn't call her, then she wouldn't have to hear the news of Gloria's baby and Nathan's joy. How many times did she have to be reminded of what she'd lost, and Nathan had gained? Didn't she deserve those things too?

"I see," Seth answered, rain dripped down the sides of his face.

Violet turned and grabbed a dishtowel, tossing it in his direction. "What are you doing here? I thought we agreed, no more houses."

"There's a showing on the house today. They should be here in about fifteen minutes." He wiped his face with the towel.

"You have to at least give me a twenty-four-hour notice."

Seth sighed, tossed the towel on the counter, and stepped closer. "Let's not play this game, Violet. You and I both know whether you had a twenty-four-hour notice or not that you have no intention of making this easy on anyone, especially yourself."

She planted her fist on her jean-clad hips and glared at him. As she opened her mouth to speak, he held his finger to her lips. "You've obviously been crying. Why I don't know, but I do know that letting go of something that has become a part of you is extremely difficult, and I can appreciate the struggle you're going through."

"Spare me the lecture. You don't know anything about what I'm going through." A clap of thunder caused her to quake inside, and she knew Seth sensed her fear as he laid his hand on her arm.

"You're afraid of thunderstorms."

Her throat tightened. "Does that surprise you?"

"I don't know. You're a very tough shell to crack," Seth said.

Violet took off her apron, and a long strand of hair released from the twisted knot at the back of her neck. "I'm guessing you want me to leave now." She'd rather drive through the storm than sit and wait for it to end.

"I won't kick you out. Chances are in this weather. They may not show up."

Just like Kyle, on her wedding day.

That night, Violet found it difficult to sleep. Her heart and her mind had gone to war with each other. She fought desperately to put them both to rest, and by morning she still hadn't slept a wink. When she opened her bedroom closet, her wedding gown greeted her.

Beneath clear plastic hung folds of white velvet with pearl and ribbon trim, a makeover of her mother's gown. She fingered the pearl necklace her mother had loaned her to go with it. Inside her jewelry box were the blue sapphire earrings she'd received for her birthday that year, and the old penny tucked into the white satin shoes she'd intended to walk down the aisle wearing.

It all seemed as if a dream, a beautiful, short-lived dreamed.

Her brother had taken it away. The dream belonged to

him now. Regret swelled up inside her. One of them had to end up lonely. Nathan would never have met Gloria if Kyle hadn't gone away. If she hadn't sent him away.

She plucked a shirt from the closet and dressed.

Kyle and Nathan were inseparable since childhood. She figured they'd been best friends since middle school, maybe before that. There never seemed to be a place for a straggling little sister who always got them into trouble. The more she brought up memories of Kyle and Nathan as best friends, the more she felt him slipping away from her.

She pulled on a pair of boots and a jacket. Trudging outside in the frosted air and whitewashed ground, she headed for the garage.

On cold days like this, Kyle would always find a way to make her forget the cold and warm her with laughter. They'd huddle together and watch NASCAR, trying to predict the lead car. On some occasions, she and Kyle would visit the youth centers. Many times, Kyle would go speak with the teenagers about overcoming life's obstacles and rising to their full potential.

She stepped into the empty garage and halted. Her heart stopped, and her mind raced a mile a minute. It was gone!

Frantically, she paced around the garage for clues. Nothing appeared out of place. The doors were locked, and no damage visible.

From the wall, a life-size poster board cut out of Kyle in his racing uniform waved at her. Slowly, the beat of her heart resumed. Rationality brought with it deep grief and over-whelming agitation. Relief came slowly to ease her tension as anger rose in her belly and burned like fire.

There was only one person with access to this garage beside herself, and now Kyle's car no longer graced its walls.

∿

"There's been an offer on the house."

Violet rocked back in her chair as if he'd slapped her. "So, what are you saying?"

"Your house is being sold. You have forty-five days to vacate the premises."

She felt a cinch around her chest tighten and doubled over, unable to breathe. In an instant, Seth stood beside her.

"Somebody, get me some water!" Seth called out.

Violet shook her head. Sniffing quick breaths and squeezing her eyes shut against the black spots invading her vision. She fought to regain control, taking slow deep breaths. She opened her eyes, and her gaze found Seth's brown ones filled with concern. She clung to his arm.

As if she needed to hear the words, she asked, "The offer can be refused, right?"

She should have known this would happen. Who did she think she was fooling? Nobody but herself, she thought, her nose burned and her throat constricted with the onset of tears. She didn't expect it to happen this soon, nor had she expected him to call her into his office either. This is what he'd wanted to talk to her about?

The raven-haired women came in the office and handed Seth a paper cup.

Violet waved the offer of a drink away. Her grip remained on his arm.

Seth set the cup on the edge of his desk and sat on his heels beside her. "The other party has accepted the offer, and they're coming in today to sign the papers."

Violet's blood ran cold. Her heartbeat loudly in her ears. She prayed. This couldn't be happening to her. *Not one more thing*, she begged God, *not the house too.*

"There has to be something I can do," she whispered, her voice hoarse.

Seth cupped her chin in his hand, "You can sign the papers."

Hope burst from within her heart. "If I don't sign the papers, they can't sell!"

"All you would be doing is prolonging the inevitable. Do you really want to drag this out?"

She sniffled. Seth had a point. Obviously, God hadn't been listening, or *He* wouldn't be doing this.

Seth stood and pulled a folder from the other side of his desk. "I can call your mother if you want."

She lifted her gaze and saw him hold the phone in one hand and a folder in the other. "My mother is the last person I'd ever call." There she'd said it.

"Nathan, then?"

She remembered, at eight, falling out of a tree. Nathan had picked her up, but it had been Kyle who'd been the first to sign her arm cast. The person she needed right now would never be there to pick her up and make everything better again.

"Please ..." She held her hand to her head, feeling the tension crawl up her neck and spread across her temples. "Let's just get this over with."

Seth slid the papers and a pen toward her on the desk.

Violet reached to pick up the paper. Her hand trembled.

She scanned the papers over and over again, but she couldn't read a single word. "I will sign these papers, and this will be the beginning of the end of my life."

She felt Seth's arm around her shoulders, and his silent presence brought her comfort.

How would she find the strength to go forward without the daily reminders of Kyle's presence in her life? As she wiped away the tears and gazed at the papers, she stifled back a sob.

Seth held out a handkerchief.

Violet dried her tears and blew her nose. "I suppose I should get this over with."

"We don't have to do this right now."

"Yes, I do."

Seth handed her the pen. Taking a deep breath, she willed her hand to steady as she scribbled her name across the lines of the sales agreement.

She dotted her 'I's and crossed the 'T,' and handed the papers back to Seth. She clutched her stomach as suddenly it lurched.

"You don't have to go through this alone." He took her hands into the warmth of his own. "Let me be your friend, Violet. Let me help you."

She hadn't had a friend in a very long time. She felt a lump form in her throat.

"What do you say? Friends?"

His eyes locked with her gaze, and she felt herself start to smile. "Friends."

He gave her hands a gentle squeeze. "Great. How about lunch?"

"Lunch?"

"Sure, why not?" he asked.

"I don't know where to start?" Her gaze drifted back to the papers in his hand.

"We'll start with lunch. Then it's time for us to find a place for you, all your own."

Grabbing her bag, she stood and waited for him as he filed the papers in his desk. "I'm not sure ..."

"We're friends now, remember? Friends are always there for each other." He placed his hands on her shoulders. "Now, how about that lunch?"

Violet clutched her stomach and shook her head.

"Then let me take you somewhere. Where do you want to go?"

Violet thought long and hard about his question and then said, "The place on Main Street works." She hoped Gwen still worked there. It felt like forever since she last saw one of her old friends before Kyle died.

7

Hot apple cider and fresh-baked pumpkin pie scented the house as Violet arrived, twenty minutes late for Thanksgiving dinner.

"You made it," Elaine embraced her. "I was afraid you weren't going to come."

"What? And miss all the fun?" Violet said as she shrugged off her jacket and handed it to her mother. She left her pink scarf wrapped around her neck and draped down over the shoulder of her ivory sweater.

"Everyone's already seated. Nathan was about to give the blessing." Violet followed Elaine into the dining room.

"I take it there's no baby."

Gloria rubbed her stomach, "False alarm. The doctor called them Braxton Hicks, but those contractions sure felt real."

Nathan, seated beside Gloria, reached over and ran his thumb down Gloria's cheek. Violet turned her head away, and Seth grinned.

"I saved you a seat." He stood, pulling out the chair next to him. Elaine busied herself by fussing over the turkey and turning a pie slightly to the left before taking a seat on the lower end of the table.

"Dear Heavenly Father, please help us to remember the things we are thankful for today, and see the light beyond the darkness on the days when all seems to be lost. Today, we are gathered together as a family and thankful for the friends who could join us. Thank you for the blessing of this meal we are about to partake and those unable to be here. Watch over my wife as she prepares to give birth to our first child. Thank you, Lord, for our Mother, that you would continue to keep her in good health. And thank you, Lord, for appointing Seth to help Violet transition from one home to another; may you guide Seth and give him strength in the days to come." And they all said, "Amen."

Seth looked up, peered around the table, and then glanced at Violet. He could see the fatigue hanging off her like a hundred-pound sack of flour. She was tired. He knew she would complain and he'd come prepared.

"What are you doing *here*?" she whispered.

"Your mother invited me."

"That's Elaine," Violet said. "She'd invite every homeless man off the street and give him a meal if she could."

Nathan reached for the turkey, and Elaine spooned sweet potatoes on her plate. Violet fussed over the folds of her linen napkin, but her face told him she hadn't gone unaffected by Nathan's prayer. Silently, he lifted her to God in his own prayer. He found it strange Nathan wouldn't have mentioned his own sister and her struggles.

Perhaps this was just another piece of the puzzle that made-up Violet. He cleared his throat. "Bread?"

Violet glanced over at him, hesitated, and then took a piece.

Gloria shifted in her seat, and Nathan paused from pouring his wife a drink. Violet's eyes lowered to her plate, and he reached over for her glass and filled it with water from a nearby pitcher.

"Oh, Gloria, are you not feeling well?" Elaine asked.

"It's only some back pain, it comes, and it goes."

Nathan's brow wrinkled as he watched his wife. "Do you want a pillow for your back?"

"Would you like some green beans?" Seth held out the casserole dish in Violet's direction. She smiled at him, her eyes fixed on Gloria, and he spooned green beans on her plate. "Turkey?" he offered.

"Are you having contractions again?" Nathan asked his wife.

Seth felt himself grow impatient. He stuck his fork into a piece of turkey, but Violet held up her hand and shook her head, "I don't eat meat."

"She doesn't eat a lot of things." Elaine looked across the table at him. "I try and try ..."

Violet rolled her eyes and, as if to make a point, stabbed her fork into the green beans. She stuffed her mouth and chewed.

"We have a few more weeks yet," he heard Gloria reply. "They're not consistent like Doctor Raymond said they'd be."

"There's no sense in getting all worked up." Elaine held her fork in mid-air and glared over her sweet potatoes at Violet with a challenging gleam in her eye. "Are you drinking enough? You could just be dehydrated." She turned back to Gloria.

"I still think we should call Dr. Raymond." Nathan shifted in his chair and took a drink.

"At least it's Dr. Raymond and not Doc Harrison," Elaine said.

"He is the one who set my nose." He saw Violet wince and felt bad for bringing it up. A few moments later, Seth felt something brush beside his leg and glanced down.

"That's Marco, he's Nathan's lazy mutt," Violet said,

taking the last bite of her green beans. "Polo is around here somewhere, probably licking out a dish in the kitchen."

Seth reached down and stroked the Beagle's head. The dog laid its snout on his knee and stared up at him with glossy brown eyes. "I know how you feel," he muttered.

Violet sipped her water. She'd styled her hair so that it feathered around her oval face, unlike the ponytail or bun he saw most often. Smudges of dark purple circled her eyes just beneath her thin layer of foundation. She might think she could fool everyone else, but she couldn't trick Seth.

One tough bird, Violet. She stuck to her commitments. He liked that about her. If only he knew that her faith was that strong, too.

"Nathan, stop pestering your wife and let her eat." Elaine pointed her fork at Nathan, "Gloria knows her body if she needs a doctor; it's her call."

"Thank you, Mom," Gloria winced. "I've been telling him that all day."

"If they don't go away by morning, I'm calling," Nathan said.

Seth never thought he'd say this, "You want to grab dessert somewhere else?"

Before Violet could answer, Gloria interrupted. "How is the house hunt coming along?" She nudged away Nathan's hands on her belly.

"I told her she could move in with me. Her room is just sitting up there empty," Elaine said.

"Violet is a grown woman, she needs to be out on her own." Nathan pointed his fork in Violet's direction. "Don't you think, Seth?"

"I live with my grandmother." Inwardly, he winced. Good going, Jones, women are always impressed by men who lived with their grandmothers.

"See, there's no reason Violet shouldn't move back home."

Seth could think of one, and by Violet's expression, he guessed she had a few objections of her own.

"I'm not moving in with you, Elaine. I'm fine just where I'm at." Violet crossed her arms.

"What about the sale of the house?" Gloria asked, rubbing her belly.

"She's got forty-two days until the closing date." Seth leaned forward in his chair. "By then, we should be able to find something suitable, I'm sure."

After dinner, Nathan gathered up the plates and headed for the kitchen. The old mangy dog followed behind him. Seth assisted Gloria as she prepared to stand up from the table.

"I'll help," Violet said, gathering platters of food. Elaine touched Gloria's shoulder. The look in Elaine's eyes told him to stay put. Her gaze cast a warning signal between them.

Violet balanced a pile of dishes in one arm and pushed the swinging door into the kitchen with the other. A quivering smile appeared on Gloria's lips.

Slowly, Elaine counted down from twenty under her breath. Before she reached one, Seth heard the sound of glass smashing in the kitchen.

The door flapped closed behind her, and Violet extended her arms holding out the dirty dishes from dinner. Nathan's sleeves were rolled up, and hot soapy water filled the sink behind him.

Nathan turned at the sound of the door. He reached out for the dirty plates, but Violet planted her feet on the ceramic tiled floor and held them just out of reach.

"Where is it?"

Nathan frowned. "What?"

"You know exactly *what*. I stopped by the storage shed on my way here, it's not there." Violet took a deep breath to calm her rising anxiety. "You're the only person, other than me, that has access to the garage."

Nathan turned back to the sink. "I moved it. You would have had to move it anyway with the sale of the house."

She wrestled with her heart. "Who gave you the right to make decisions for me?" She gripped the dirty dishes in her hand.

"Go lie down, Polo," Nathan instructed the dog at his feet. "Leave it be, it's fine where it's at." He turned back around to face her.

"You had no right taking it." Her voice rose. She felt close to tears.

"What are you going to do with it, Twig?" he asked.

"Don't call me by that silly nickname." She glared at him. "It doesn't matter what I do with it. It belongs to me. If you don't give it back, I'll ..."

"You'll what, *Twig*? Call Sheriff Brady?" Nathan shot back.

"Where is it?" That's all she wanted to know. It was the last thing she had to hold on to—Kyle's stock car.

"You know for a moment, you had me fooled. When are you going to give up the façade and let go?"

The weight of the dishes made her arms, like her bottom lip, quiver. Two years, she'd waited. Time heals all wounds of the heart, but now she felt she couldn't be more wrong. "If you have any idea what that car means to me, you'll return it, pronto."

"I'm not giving back the car," he said.

"I suppose I should have expected *you* to say that. After all, you've stolen everything else from me."

"No, I haven't." He took a step towards her. "I'm not the one forcing the house sale."

"No, but you'll do nothing to help me stop it."

"Twig ..." he took a step towards her.

Violet shook her head, tears threatened to spill. "You've

taken everything away from me. *I* was supposed to be the one who got married. It should be *me* sitting in there pregnant, not *her*. Not *you*!"

Her body quaked.

"You're not the only one who lost something that day," he said softly. "I lost my best friend, remember?"

Her vision blurred, and the dishes wavered in her hands.

"Don't ever think for one moment that I don't miss him, but I've found my peace. I've accepted God had other plans for our lives. It's time you did, too."

She focused on breathing. He stepped closer. Did he think she would just forgive him and go on as if nothing had ever happened? She shook her head. She couldn't ever forget, and she'd never forgiven him. She didn't need him.

"No one is punishing you or trying to steal your life, Twig. Gloria, Mother, and I—we all care about you."

At the mention of Gloria, Violet drew rigid. "You don't care about me. You have a wife, a baby, and now you want to take away the only thing I have left of the man I love." Misery, sorrow, pain, they flooded her like the riptide that stole Kyle from her life. She caught a sob in her throat, refused to let Nathan see her cry, and held her breath.

"A car can't make you happy or give you a life," Nathan said.

"I want it back."

"Then you'll have to find your heart first," he said.

Maybe, just maybe, she didn't know where to find her heart anymore. All feeling had shed from her the day she buried Kyle.

But somewhere, deep in the recesses of her heart, she felt a spark ignite, and it didn't have anything to do with the handsome real estate agent trying to sell her house. No, she decided, it had more to do with her new friend, Seth. So what if he just happened to be the same real estate agent who promised to help her find a new home.

Nathan reached out to her and touched her arm. Startled, she dropped the dishes. Violet jumped back as they smashed on the floor. Nathan's expression, she was sure, mirrored her own shock.

"Violet ..."

She turned and fled out the door. As it swung open, she ran into Seth. Instantly, his arms went around her. She saw her mother and Gloria, both frowning. Both staring at her.

She shoved Seth away and ran from the house. Outside in the brisk November chill, she stood in the driveway.

She wrapped her arms around herself. Tears of desperation soaked her face. She closed her eyes and prayed like she never prayed before, pouring every last drop of bitterness and resentment she held. Why did being around her brother always have to cause her pain?

She felt the brush of fur under her chin. She looked over her shoulder at Seth. He wrapped her coat around her shoulders from behind.

"I thought you might be cold," he said.

She wiped the tears from her sodden cheeks. Why did it seem that every time Seth came near, she cried? She didn't get weepy-eyed in front of strangers or her family. Perhaps because they were friends now, that it made a difference.

He wrapped his arms around her, and she leaned back against him, allowing her body to relax. She felt drained. Violet let out everything she had held inside for so long. Feeling like an empty shell of herself, delicate and ready to crack. She allowed Seth to hold her, too exhausted to push away.

Small flakes of snow fell from the sky. She held out a hand, watched as one by one they touched her palm and melted. She laughed.

"What's so funny?" Seth asked, turning her around to face him.

"When we were kids, we'd stick out our tongues and try to

catch snowflakes." She giggled. "One time, Kyle dared Nathan to stick his tongue on our light pole." She pointed across the snow-covered yard.

"And did he?" Seth asked.

"Oh, yeah," Violet said. "Dad was so mad. Once they got Nathan unstuck, we all got a lecture for weeks about jumping off bridges and using common sense. But after that, Nathan and Kyle were always finding new things to dare each other with." Her voice trailed off.

"Why don't we take a drive, I'm sure we can find a place with some warm pie and hot coffee that's open today."

She gazed up into his face. His cheeks and nose were red from the cold, and his eyes radiated kind warmth that aroused a flutter in her heart. "I'd prefer lemon pie."

"Then lemon it is," he said.

She caught the subtle hint of pink around his arm and an arched a brow. "Oh, I believe this is yours." He pulled her handbag down off his shoulder and handed it to her. "I thought you might need it,"

"You know, pink isn't that bad of a color on you," she said.

As they sat inside the lake view diner, Violet rested her chin in her hands and sighed. He'd driven them over an hour west, away from town and into the more rural area of Shelby County.

She loved Hidden Hills, with its small-town charm and old-fashion hospitality. Ever since she could remember, she'd spent weekends and summers out at Shelby Lake, fishing, skating, or lounging in a boat with her family.

She'd come to look forward to those times when she, Nathan, and Kyle would hang out on the dock. Hidden Hills had become as much a part of her as Kyle had been. If only Nathan hadn't moved into their father's cabin, then maybe …

"What can I get you, folks?"

Violet glanced over at the waitress. Her broad white-toothed grin couldn't hide the pale complexion or dark rings around the waitress's eyes. Around them, the diner seemed empty, except for a few local patrons and the sounds of rattling pans coming from inside the kitchen.

They'd missed the lunch crowd if there had been one. Violet couldn't imagine a holiday focused around family that they would have much business.

"We're out of turkey," said the waitress, pulling out her pad and pen.

"We're here just for the pie," Seth said, giving Violet a wink.

"Then you've come to the right place, we've got the best pie around, just ask anyone in town."

"Is it still made from scratch?" Violet asked.

"As always." The waitress beamed. "Was up all night helping make them myself."

"I like the sound of that," Seth rubbed his hands together, "What do you have?"

Violet cast her gaze outside the window, overlooking the lake. She spied a young couple skating. The woman's arm went around the man's waist and his arm around the woman's shoulders. It seemed like an eternity since she'd put on a pair of skates and glided across the ice.

"We're all out of pumpkin, but there's apple, lemon, and cherry left."

"Lemon for two," Seth ordered.

Violet turned away from the window and looked at Seth. He seemed content sitting there and watching her from the other side of their booth. If she didn't know better, she'd think he had feelings for her.

She chided herself, Seth couldn't possibly feel more than mere friendship towards her, or could he? A sudden ache formed in her chest, a yearning. Having Seth around dredged up emotions inside her that she'd managed to keep locked away, until now. She couldn't afford to ache for something that could never be.

"Seems like a nice family-owned establishment," Seth said.

"You won't find any fast-food franchises around here like you do in the bigger cities, and the locals prefer it that way."

"Seems to me with all the tourists coming in during the seasons that there would be a few closer to town."

"Is that where you grew up?" Violet leaned back against the vinyl seat.

"Richmond, then my grandfather passed on, and we moved to Hidden Hills."

Which would explain why he'd only been attending the same church as her family for the past few years.

"They say you can take a boy from the city, but you can't ever take the city away from the boy."

Seth grinned, "City, small town, it makes no difference to me. A home is more than its location. It's the people who create a covenant in your heart."

"Now you sound like my family."

Seth's features grew soft, and the laugh lines beside his eyes flattened. He appeared as if he were going to lean forward, but as the waitress returned, pouring them each a cup of coffee, he leaned further away.

Violet wrapped her cold hands around the cup. "I suppose I should thank you."

"For the pie?"

"For rescuing me from my family." She stared down at the dark liquid in her cup.

"Mind if I ask what happened back there?"

"You wouldn't understand."

"Let me guess, it's complicated?"

She couldn't hold back the smile on her lips. "You're getting to know me too well."

"Apparently not well enough," he said. "You never cease to amaze me."

Violet blushed. "My family seems to think they know what's best for me and my life. They just want me to forget that yesterday ever happened, pretend that Kyle never existed, and I can't do that."

Violet reached over and poured creamer into her coffee. She spotted the waitress, making her way toward them again. Somewhere behind her, she heard the bell above the door ring.

"You can't blame them for wanting what's best for you. I'd think your mother, most of all, would want you to be happy."

Feeling the hairs on her neck rise, Violet said, "How would you know? You're a grown man still living with his grandmother, right?"

She watched the pained expression in his eyes, and his features hardened. She bit her lip.

"Yeah, I suppose your right."

The waitress returned with a small plate of lemon pie. "This is the last piece we've got left. You can split it, or I can get you something else," she set the slice of pie between them.

"I suppose this means we'll have to share."

"You can have it. I'm fine with coffee," Seth said.

"Suit yourself." The waitress sashayed off to another table.

As she picked up her fork, Violet hesitated in cutting the slice of pie. "I'm sorry. I shouldn't have said that about you living with your grandmother."

"No, you're right. What would I know about families? My mother left me when I was seven." He took a sip of his coffee.

"You did say something about that, didn't you?"

"Yeah, my mother had big dreams and little ambition towards motherhood. She felt having a kid weighed her down from getting what she wanted."

"An actress?"

"A husband."

"Oh," Violet blanched. "I never think before I say things I shouldn't."

"As you said, I'm a big boy. I forgave my mother years ago."

When she'd finished with her pie, Seth took care of the bill, and they walked outside. "Why don't we go for a walk before I take you back?"

Going back was the last place she'd hoped he'd take her.

8

They walked along the frozen lakeshore. Seth slipped Violet's hand into the bend of his arm. As the evening sky dimmed, skaters stepped off the ice.

One thing he never learned was how to ice skate.

Skaters spun, gliding around in figure eights, and couples took that last lap before retreating for hot chocolate. Violet's face radiated with her pink, wind-burnt cheeks and red nose.

"Come on," Violet tugged on his hand, "Let's go skating!"

Her childlike enthusiasm enlightened him, but as she dragged him towards the small skate rental shack, it fell short at convincing him to go out on the ice.

"You've got about an hour left." The clerk said when Violet inquired about skates.

"What size are you?" she turned to him.

"Um ..." he glanced down at his feet and then at her again. "Why don't you go on, I'll watch."

She tilted her head and laughed, "You can't skate, can you?"

"No, I've never been on the ice, except maybe to fish with a client."

"Well, there is always a first time." She grinned, her eyes twinkling.

"I don't know." He looked out at the lake, where several skaters raced across the ice. "You'll have to teach me."

"I'll even let you hold on to me." She promised with a sweet smile.

Liking that idea, he gave the clerk his shoe size and found a bench nearby. Violet sat on the bench with her skates tossed beside her. Seth crouched in front of her. For a moment, she didn't move. Didn't breathe. Seth took her foot, slipping off her boot.

"Violet? Are you okay?"

She'd gone pale. "It's just—no one has ever done that for me."

"Done what?"

"You know … make me feel …"

Cherished? Special? Seth wanted to say.

Protected.

He wanted to reply but thought best to savor this moment with silence.

The color returned to her face. Her glowing expression told him he'd made progress.

Wobbly, like a newborn fawn, Seth tried to gain his legs as they stepped towards the ice. Violet moved smoothly onto the frozen lake and held her hands out towards him.

"Why don't you go for a round or two while I get the hang of this on my own?" he suggested. Violet grinned, shrugged, and skated away.

He watched her graceful movements as she circled around the small area of the lake with the other skaters, like a pro. She weaved around skaters and did a jump spin halfway around the skate area.

When no one was looking, he stepped out onto the ice. His feet slid out from under him. Air rushed from his lungs as he landed flat on his back.

Seth lay sprawled out on the ice and staring up at the sky. A vision of an angel appeared over him.

He blinked as a pair of gloved hands came into view. With soft pink hues and fragrances of pine and flowery perfume, Violet stood over him.

"Need a hand?"

He shook his head, attempted to gain his feet, but one skate slid in front of him, and his other foot slid back. Violet caught him by the arm, but he landed in an awkward split on the ice.

He grimaced. "Thanks."

"Use the pick at the end of your blade to hold still," she tipped her foot to demonstrate. "Then stand up."

She held him by the elbow. One foot at a time, he put his feet together, bent his knees, and straightened himself. He wobbled and clutched on to her. Looking her in the eye, he felt the back of his neck grow warm.

"Steady now?"

"I think I got it." He released her, but at the slight movement, he rocked back and grabbed for her again. She took hold of his hand. "Just hold on to me."

"I'm a lot bigger than you are."

"Then, I wouldn't fall again if I were you." She teased. "Come on, it's just like when you were a kid and would slide your feet on the ice."

Seth tried to focus on her face, focus on moving his feet, and soon she guided him out farther onto the frozen lake. How could he ever tell her that she'd etched a tiny place in his heart?

"See, isn't this fun?"

Fun, had nothing to do with it. If he weren't careful, Seth would end up falling flat on his face, or worse—on his back again—in front of Violet.

"Do this often?" he managed between watching his feet and glancing at her face.

"When I was a kid, my dad brought us here all the time, and I could skate circles around him and Nathan." She frowned. Her forehead furrowed.

"You're blessed to have a brother so close to you."

"I wouldn't call it blessed," Violet turned and skated backward to face him. "More like plagued."

She didn't know what a good thing she had. All during his childhood, he'd prayed that one day, his mother would come back for him. He'd asked God for a brother, someone to play with on rainy afternoons when Pop slept in his easy chair, and Gram stitched blankets for the homeless.

He imagined a big mansion on a hill, just like his mother always promised him. There was a dog at the foot of his bed and laughter throughout the house. He'd search the papers every Sunday, cutting out pictures of the most prominent homes and hung them above his bed.

Thanks to his Grandmother, he'd found his mansion.

"Watch out!"

A boy in a blue puffed coat bumped Seth in pursuit of being chased. Seth jerked back. His arms shot out, and he tilted like a veering plane, leaning forward for a nosedive. Violet latched onto him, attempting to pull him back to a straight standing position, but the kids caught him off guard, and he tumbled forward, taking her down alongside him.

Facedown on the ice, Seth heard laughter. He turned his head and discovered Violet's legs entwined with his. They looked like a soft pretzel stuck to the ice. Violet laughed.

He grunted. He hadn't scored any points in the suave section for this stunt. Still, Violet laughed. Painstakingly, he eased himself up on his hands and looked down at her.

Her hat had fallen off, and her hair spilled out over the top of the ice like gold silk. He stared into her eyes, and her laughter died away. His heart wouldn't stop pounding, and he felt the sudden sizzle of electricity between them.

She'd felt it, too. Leaning down closer, her breath caught, and her gaze drifted to his lips.

"Hey, Mister!" A spray of ice showered them as several pairs of skates skidded to a stop beside them. "Are you all right?"

Seth tore his gaze from Violet and looked up in the direction of three young boys. She scooted out from beneath him, breathless. "I think it's time for you to take me home."

She looked at herself in the mirror. A train wreck, she believed that's how her mother had described her appearance a few weeks ago. It still applied now. She'd tossed, turned, and rolled around until her bed linens threatened to swallow her whole by morning. Every time she closed her eyes, she saw Seth's face leaning in close, and her heart sped rapidly in her chest.

She splashed cold water on her face. Bloodshot eyes stared back at her. No make-up in the world could cover that, but a pair of sunglasses might. How could she expect to sell her natural made cosmetics if her customers saw her like this? It was bad for business, like the models she worked with occasionally each year at the car expo, here today and gone tomorrow.

She picked up a towel and patted her face dry. The last few days she'd spent more time in Seth's company then she'd spent with her family in an entire year. She'd chosen the company of a stranger over her own family. But, Seth wasn't a stranger. He was her friend.

She took a deep breath and waited for the gut-wrenching pain to curl in her stomach, but none came.

She powdered her face.

Whenever she came around him, he made her feel unsettled, off-balance, and annoyed. She hadn't felt anything like this for years until he'd come along. She'd found herself lying on her back and staring up at his face, wishing he'd kiss her.

For days, she'd been trying to sort out her feelings and comprehend how she could yearn for the very thing that had robbed her life of joy.

She smeared a touch of peach gloss on her lips and smacked them together.

The first day of December brought sunshine and glistening treetops from the world beyond her colonial windows.

There were twenty-nine houses on her street. In only seven of those homes did she recognize the residents.

This was a season she favored above all else. Only in the winter, could she expect long quiet stretches of time when one could savor being by oneself. Winter brought a serenity that no other season brought, privacy.

She'd had that once.

She intended to have it again.

As long as she remained alone, no one else she cared about could ever be hurt.

Once upon a time, she, Kyle, and Nathan never went anywhere without each other. Except Nathan had convinced her a few days before the wedding to stay home. "One last adventure," Nathan promised.

She should have never agreed to stay home. When the call came just two days before her wedding, her mother referred to the accident as "an act from God."

Nathan had survived.

Search me O God and know my heart. A calming peace settled over her as she brushed her hair back from her face.

Forty-five minutes later, she opened the door to Smith and Jones Realty. The raven-haired woman greeted her, whom she recognized from the day at the hospital.

"I'm looking for Seth Jones," Violet said, clutching a folder in front of her.

"One moment." The woman picked up the receiver on the desk in front of her. "Someone to see you."

Violet listened.

"Alright," she smiled and turned to Violet. "He'll be with you in a minute."

Violet stood and looked around. Seth's office appeared laid out like a home with each room a different office. She didn't spot Seth in any of them and remembered from the last time she was there, that his office was around the corner.

"I'm Tracy, by the way. Is Seth showing you a property today?" Tracy asked, filing a broken nail.

"Not today." Violet's expert eye appraised the woman's appearance. The bright pink sheen of her lips and eyes were too distracting on the woman's round face. "You may want to try a warmer tone of blush and neutralize your eyes," Violet said.

"Excuse me?" Tracy paused from filing her nail.

"Those shades of eye shadow and lip gloss are entirely too bright for you."

"You don't say." Tracy looked darkly at her.

Violet reached down in her bag and pulled out a few sample packets. "I own Violaceae's natural beauty care products and cosmetics. Here, try these. You'll be amazed at the difference when you look in the mirror."

Tracy's arms crossed, "I like pink."

"So do I, but it doesn't mean it can always be flattering," Violet said as she held out the samples. "Your dark hair and brown eyes make warm and neutral tones more flattering to your complexion. Add a sheen of pink to your lips, but just try these and tell me what you think."

"I'm sure Tracy would love to have you chat about that stuff all day, but I believe you came to see me?" Seth said from behind her.

"Just when it was starting to get interesting." Tracy made a face at Seth and smiled back at Violet. "Warm and neutral? Huh?"

Violet turned toward Seth.

"Do you always solicit people?"

"No, if I did, I would have told you to get a haircut," Violet said.

He scowled. "Are you offering?"

"I could grab my case and do it now." She followed him as he led her back to his office.

"The traveling beautician."

"I prefer making beauty products, but sometimes the job calls for styling too." She fluttered her lashes at him.

Seth frowned, ran his hand through his hair, and then shook his head. "I'm sure you didn't come here because you thought I needed a haircut."

"No, but I don't mind."

He seemed to consider her offer, then reached forward and tapped the folder in her hand. "What's this?"

She took a deep breath. "I've made my decision. If I can't stay at my house on Oak Street, then I'd like to be as close to the lake as I can afford."

Seth sat on the corner of his desk, speechless. Perhaps God had given him that miracle he'd asked for, after all.

"I've chosen a house." Violet giggled, the joy overflowing from her like liquid from a shaken can of soda.

"This is sooner than I expected." He regarded her. This wasn't the woman who'd sat in her home and refused to cooperate. Nor was this the woman who'd sobbed in his office a few weeks ago, and now he wasn't sure what he was up against. He leaned back and braced himself as he tried to regroup.

"I've only got thirty days left, and I'm not moving in with my mother," she said.

It made sense, but he still couldn't understand why she harbored such ill-favored feelings towards her mother. "You may end up needing a place for a week or two between house transitions."

His gaze fell to the soft wisps of hair down the sides of her face. He liked it down; pulled back, it felt severe and made her seem unapproachable.

"I'll make other arrangements," she handed him the folder. "I've written up my offer, and everything is in here."

He ignored the folder. "Would it be so terrible? Living with your mother?"

She blinked, stared at him for the longest second, and sighed. She plopped down in the nearest chair. "Let's just say, when I needed my mother, she wasn't there for me, and how would you feel if your grandmother tried to direct your life the way Elaine does mine?"

"We all make mistakes, Violet. We may never forget what others have done to us, but we can forgive them."

He could appreciate how she felt. As a teenager, he felt suffocated by his grandmother's authority over his life. That's when he'd taken his first drink and fallen from grace.

He recalled the struggle to reclaim his life, the support, and gentle, persistent persuasions from his grandparents. He imagined Violet had suffocated under her family's attempts to drag her back from her grief and into the presence of the living. Only their efforts pushed her away more than they pulled her closer to that goal.

"Some things are too hard to forget." She reached out and handed him the folder again.

Their fingers brushed as he took the folder. She'd printed out a copy of the home's detail report, scratched out the listed price, and wrote in her own. Ironically, she'd chosen the same house he would have picked.

But the house was inconsequential. Would his friendship with Violet be over the day she signed the purchase papers?

He prayed not for his own sake more than Violet's.

"I printed it off the internet, so that means it hasn't been sold yet, right?"

"I don't see any reason why it would be if you were able to pull it up online." He scooted around his desk and sat in his chair. A few strokes at the keyboard of his computer confirmed the home had not yet been contracted.

He raked his hands through his hair and leaned back in his chair. "You're on your own on this one. I'm afraid I can't help you or act as your agent due to a conflict of interest."

"Conflict of interest?"

"This house is listed by my agency."

"You said it was a bank foreclosure." She was on her feet in seconds.

"Sit down, it is."

She tilted her head and glared at him, easing herself back down into her chair.

"Tracy is the listing agent." He explained. "Since we are both brokers of this agency, and based on our relationship, it would be a conflict of interest for me to stand by you as your agent."

He watched her frown and fidget.

"Then, where do you stand?" She bit her lip.

Seth leaned forward. "I stand by *you* first and foremost, as your friend. I can still write up the offer and hand it to Tracy, but I can't give you any advice on negotiations." For a few seconds, he held his breath.

A slow smile curved on her lips. "I can handle that, as long as you never stop being my friend."

Relief flooded him and sobered him at the same time. Violet's friendship wasn't like any other friendship he had; he wanted more. He wanted her to trust him, to confide in him, and to be with him always. But he feared if Violet knew his intentions, she'd flee. He'd just gotten used to the idea himself.

9

Violet heard the truck pull into the driveway and peeked out the window. Strapped on a dolly behind an old Ford pickup, sat Kyle's car. She grabbed her jacket and went outside. Nathan slid out of the truck cab with Marco pressing his wet nose against the windshield.

"Gloria was afraid you'd have me arrested, and I'd be in jail when she went into labor."

Her boots crunched in the snow. "I knew you would bring it back, eventually."

"The manager of the storage facility contacted me a while back. Robert Freeman had been there making inquiries, trying to get into your unit."

She gasped, not because of Robert Freeman, that was nothing new, but because Nathan had Kyle's car far longer than she realized.

"It's probably not a good idea to put it back in storage."

"He'll try again," Violet said. The Freeman family was relentless. They wanted one thing, and they'd do anything to get it. The house didn't matter to them.

It was the car. It had always been about the car. Now that Kyle was gone, his younger brother, Scott, was next in line to drive for the Freeman racing crew. Only Violet knew, from Kyle, that Scott had no ambition towards driving, and now he used Kyle's car as an excuse not to drive. Without the car, the Freeman's didn't need a driver.

Violet didn't feel one bit of sympathy for their plight, even though everything she'd been taught about God's love told her it was wrong.

She watched as Nathan pulled back the covering and revealed the black and silver sheen of the front fender. She crossed her arms against the chill. "You love that car more than you love me," she whispered.

Nathan paused and looked over his shoulder. The front of the car sparkling in the afternoon sun, unclothed.

"What's that?" Nathan brows furrowed.

Violet's gaze moved from the car to Nathan's face. "Prove it." She stepped closer, placing her bare hand on the cold steel of the driver's side door. "That's what I said." She searched her brother's face to see if he understood. He squinted his eyes.

"Right before Daytona, prove it, prove you don't love this car more than you love me."

He nodded, "It would have been a hard choice."

That made her smile. "What can I do to make you feel loved? That's what he said." She walked around the car, her eyes locked on Nathan. "What is yours shall become mine. He deeded the car to me, put my name on the house, and vowed we'd share everything. We'd never be apart."

She stood on the other side of the car's hood. Her heart drifted away into recollected memories. "I vowed, even before our wedding day, that I'd love him for a lifetime."

"No one said you had to stop loving him." Nathan leaned against the car. "A house can't love you, and neither can a car."

Her gaze moved back to her brother, the ache in her heart felt like the cold throb in her chilled hands, exposed on this cold winter day. She bit her lip against the pain. She didn't want to argue with him, not anymore.

"Russ, over at the speedway, mentioned the car manufacturers are looking for some stock cars to feature at the car show this year. You may want to consider it. I told him he'd have to talk to you."

"Drive it around back and put it in the garage, will you?" She turned and walked away.

Cold, hard snow smashed against the back of her neck. She shrugged her neck into her coat. Icy flakes tumbled down her previously exposed neck and down her back between her jacket and sweater.

She gritted her teeth, turning back to glare at her brother. He grinned at her with his hands held behind his back. She winced as a cold trickle went down her spine.

She had no intention to pursue his childish actions with retribution, but the sloppy grin on his face made it hard to resist. She reached down in the snow, her bare hands cupping and forming a ball, and as she stood and tossed the snowball, Nathan stepped out of the way.

She watched, astonished at her own ability to propel the ball that hard and far, as the snowball hit Seth square in the chest. She covered her face with her hands, peeking through her fingers to witness his shocked expression. She hadn't seen him walking up the sidewalk.

Nathan laughed. "I guess I better get this thing in the garage and head home before any more trouble arises."

She stared at Seth through split fingers, waiting for Seth to respond. He stood, frozen like a statue, and stared at her. "If this is a bad time, I can come back."

Nathan shook his head, "I'm out of here." He looked at Violet. "Make sure you go around and unlock the garage."

She nodded, unable to find the words to respond. Another shiver erupted down her spine as the snow down her back turned to liquid, like the feeling in her knees.

Slowly, she brought down her hands and looked at Seth. Nathan slid back into his truck with Marco, who barked at the start of the truck engine.

Seth, briefcase in one hand, brushed the snow off his jacket front with the other.

"I h-have to g-go unlock the g-garage." She stammered. "The front d-door is unlocked. I'll m-meet you inside." She jogged down the side of the house and into the back yard.

She worked her cold, stiff fingers to turn the key of the lock on the garage. Inside, she hit the button for the garage door to lift.

She watched as Nathan backed the stock car up to the doorway. "Just lock it when you're done. I'll be back out later to check on it."

"You know, Russ said he could keep it until the show along with a few others he's got there," Nathan said, walking out from around the car as he undid the tire straps.

"I'd rather have it here. Right where I know where it's at."

"Just let me know when you want me to move it again."

Violet turned and walked back to the house.

"I guess it's pointless to ask what you're doing here." She entered the kitchen from the back door, stomping snow from her boots. Her cheeks were flushed from the cold, and her hands tingled as they warmed to room temperature.

"I came to see you." Seth grinned. "I would have made some hot chocolate, but I didn't want to go rummaging through your cupboards."

She spied the two coffee cups on the counter. "I don't have any. Chocolate isn't a particular fondness of mine."

Seth's eyebrows shot up, "A girl who doesn't like chocolate? Seriously?"

Maybe it was his reaction, or the way his voice hiked at the end, but either way she felt her lips spread in a wide smile. "I've got some French vanilla cappuccino or plain old coffee if you'd like."

"I thought after being pelted with snow, something warm would be nice to heat us up on the inside." Her cheeks grew warm, and she ducked her head, tucking a strand of hair behind her ear.

"Sorry about that." She bit her lip. "It should have been Nathan, not you."

"Do you always throw snowballs at your brother?"

"He started it." Nathan had a way of bringing out the worst in her at the most inopportune times.

He turned and proceeded to turn on the faucet to fill a tea kettle sitting nearby with cold water. He'd taken off his hat and gloves. His hair fell in large curls over his forehead, and he had to wipe them away to keep them from blocking his vision.

"Curious, do you and Nathan always fight?" he asked.

Violet shed her coat and shook the water drops from inside it before hanging it on a nearby chair and taking a seat at the breakfast nook.

"Not when we were kids. I used to tag along where ever he and Kyle would go, and they'd both pick on me, but we never fought, we were always close, despite our age difference. Or at least we were." She let her voice trail off.

Seth set the kettle on the stove and turned on the left front burner. He took a seat across from her. "What changed?"

She looked at him, his brown eyes focused on her, and a curl of rich brown hair touched the bridge of his nose. Unconsciously, leaning forward, she reached out and pushed it away. He didn't move; his breath caught in his throat, as did hers.

Their gazes locked and held. Violet's pulse fluttered with the scariest, most amazing, feeling she had ever experienced.

His dark eyes glazed with something she couldn't fully read.

Violet fought the surge of tenderness that overwhelmed her and threatened to melt her resistance. She allowed her hand to trace down the side of his face. Her palm pressed to his clean-shaven cheek. Her gaze fell to his lips.

"Violet …"

The kettle whistled. They jumped apart and stood up at the same time.

"I've got it," Violet said, relieved by the sudden distraction. She nearly kissed him again! Stunned to think she could, Violet was suddenly contrite.

She poured hot water into mugs and mixed in the instant cappuccino powder. All the while, she felt his eyes on her back. She willed her hands to remain steady as she carried the hot liquid to the breakfast nook. What was it about Seth Jones that made her feel like she was trembling inside?

"Milk?"

"No, thanks."

She noticed his hand on the briefcase he'd carried. She gripped her mug and set the other mug in front of him. Resenting the tea kettle for its timing, desperately, she hoped things between them could be different.

"You're here about the house."

"I thought it best if I came and gave you the news myself." He popped open his briefcase as she sat back down. He didn't appear grim, or happy, but that was probably just his business face.

She waited, staring out over his head to the kitchen window. A checkered valance hung with red string tassels. She remembered the day, she'd stood not far from where Seth sat and watched Kyle slip the material on the rod and snap it into place. How long ago that had been?

"The good news is, they've accepted your offer on the house." Her gaze pivoted back to Seth. She should be happy, but the news of her impending new home didn't bring such joy in her heart as she would have expected.

"We can arrange for closing on the same day as this place, then you wouldn't have to find a place to stay in between. However, since it's a bank repo, you'll want to have the place inspected and have the furnace running before you move in."

She didn't think about any of those things, she appreciated his thoughtfulness. "That's all? I just sign, and the place is mine?" A sickening feeling spread in her stomach. She sipped her cappuccino to make it go away.

"Not exactly, there are loan papers and down payments to discuss." Paper after paper, he took them out, explained each one, and her head felt like it was spinning. She pressed her fingers to her temples. When they were almost finished, she said, "Can we stop now, this is making my head hurt."

"Sure," Seth didn't argue. He collected the papers and put them back into his briefcase. Just like that, no pestering, no pushing, no insistence like her mother would have done. Slowly, she took a deep breath, and the throb in her temples eased. She looked out over the tabletop at Seth.

He sipped his drink and watched her with a steady gaze. "Feeling better now?"

"I keep thinking this is a dream, and I'll just wake up, and my life will be the way it was supposed to be."

"The way you wanted it to be, or the way God intended for it to be?" he asked in a soft tone of voice.

Her head snapped up, and her eyes met his. "This is not the way *we* planned it."

"No one ever plans for their life to end up the way it does. Things happen all the time that we don't plan."

She'd heard those words over and over. It wasn't fair. She'd done everything right. She'd gone to church every Sunday, read her Bible every morning, and prayed every night. None of those things were enough to save Kyle.

Her throat tightened. "If only I hadn't listened to Nathan."

"You blame your brother for Kyle's death?" Seth asked.

"Why else would have Nathan survived?"

Aghast, Seth leaned back. "You'd rather your brother was dead?"

Violet choked. It would just be like Kyle to save Nathan before himself. Nathan was a blessing through the storm. In the darkness, she'd shunned him. Blamed him. Hated him. When all she needed were strong arms to hold her up, Elaine and Nathan both failed her.

No matter how severe her heart had suffered equal blows of sorrow and faith, she'd not wish her suffering on any of her worst enemies.

"No ..." She shook her head, trying to shake away those terrible feelings seeping into her veins. Inside she grew cold, her hands trembled, and she didn't like it, this feeling that overcame her.

She blurted out, "Then why did *He* take away Kyle and give the life we'd planned to Nathan?"

Before the words were out, she regretted them. She'd harbored her feelings far too long to hold them inside anymore.

Seth took a deep breath, puckered his cheeks, and blew out hard. His hand raked through his hair. "So, this is why you and Nathan don't get along anymore, you feel as if he stole your life."

"More than you will ever know."

She had to admit, she'd felt like she'd hit a brick wall with God. She witnessed the struggle on Seth's face, his brows drew close together and creases formed on his forehead. His lips turned down.

"That would explain the baby shower, but ..."

"You didn't answer my question." She cut in, "Unless you don't have one." Seth deserved someone far better than she. Especially for him.

Seth's faith was like the most enduring fragrance she'd ever inhaled. Guilt-ridden, she became withdrawn.

"Perhaps Kyle's death is the consequence of his choice,

but God didn't take your life and give it to Nathan. Nathan
and Gloria's life was planned, just like the planning of their
child and your life, too."

"You didn't know him like I did, he was a good man, a
good Christian man who loved God with all his heart, and
God took him away. All our hopes, our dreams, our life
together ... gone. Why?"

"Those weren't the plans God has for you."

He sounded like her mother again. That wasn't the answer
she wanted to hear. He leaned towards her, not in sympathy
like all the others, but in understanding. What plights had God
put him through that he would hold such strong faith?

"I think you need to leave now," she said quietly.

"Violet ..." he reached out toward her, but she pulled
back.

"I asked you to go."

"I don't like us parting company like this ..."

"Get out!" she stood, kicked back her chair, and glared
at him.

Seth stared up at her. Blinked. Then he rose from his chair
and picked up his briefcase.

She stood, wide-legged, and prepared to battle. He walked
past her without a word. Violet watched him go out the door,
heard it shut, and sighed. Peering out the window she watched
him get into his vehicle, and for the longest time, his SUV
remained parked down the street. Did he sit and pray for her?

If he did, he wasted his time. God didn't hear prayers
where Violet was concerned, not then ... not now ... not ever.

10

"Doesn't surprise me one bit," Mary Lou Jones said as she handed Seth another strand of lights to go around the tree. "You did the right thing."

Seth hoped he had, but his grandmother's assurance brought him little relief. The more he discovered about Violet, the more he felt drawn to her friendship.

Only her friend. That was true, but he felt so much more, but he couldn't admit where his heart headed. He couldn't allow himself to confess Violet appeared attractive to him. However, her lack of faith kept him from taking their relationship any further.

He prayed God would help Violet find the true meaning of God's love and come back to her faith.

A string of lights blinked in unison, and his grandmother handed him the next strand.

His grandparents had been married for over forty-five years, and even though their skin wrinkled with age and their hair lost its color, their love for each other remained strong. He saw it each time his grandmother's gaze fell upon an old family photo, taken just a few years before his grandfather passed away.

"Here. Start this strand from the other side," his grandmother said. "I'll get the ornaments."

Seth did as she told him. He wound the lights around the tree, weaving them through the branches and remembered the first time he'd started this tradition with his grandmother. He was seven, and it was last Christmas he'd seen his mother.

She'd promised him she'd be there the next morning. They'd spend the morning in celebration under the tree and as a family. He knew there would be no gifts, for a boy like him, his mother had said so before bed.

Disappointed and heartbroken that morning, he woke up and found his mother gone. A dozen gifts sat beneath the tree, but the one gift that he would always cherish was the memory of his grandmother pulling him into her arms and telling him the story of Jesus.

Seth never knew his father, or if he did, he had no memories of the man. Pop, his grandfather, became the only male role model in his life, and the only father he came to know was the father in heaven his grandmother had taught him about.

At nine, he turned to the only place where he knew rejection wouldn't come—his heavenly father.

As the years went by, anger and bitterness infected his heart. Women were all the same, even in high school. They wanted to date only the boys with the hottest set of wheels and could buy them expensive gifts.

He'd met Myra the first year at the University of Kentucky. She'd humbled him by her situation. Like him, she worked to pay her way through school, sometimes more than one job while trying to study. But in the end, like his mother, she'd wanted more.

He drove an old beat-up Ford with a rope tied around the end of one bumper. It got him where he needed to go. He never got the opportunity to propose. He'd bought a bottle of champagne and invited her over to dinner.

That night, he sat alone with only the bottle of champagne to bring him comfort. Myra had moved on to someone better.

He should have stopped there, but one bottle of champagne lead to another, and another. He'd lost himself so completely into the drink that it took failing college and being homeless to find his way back.

"You do the honors," Mary Lou nudged him. He looked down at the angel she held in her hands. Relieved that some things don't change, like the angel that graced the top of their tree since that first Christmas long ago. He accepted it into his grasp.

With its beaded looped wings and white satin robe, he thought of Violet. He could appreciate her feelings of anger and resentment towards her family. That, and her desperate need to cling to her past.

He'd drowned in his own but had accepted the hand that pulled him out of his stoop and gotten him off the streets. An angel, who led him back to Christ and on the path to sobriety, and he'd be eternally grateful for it.

He placed the angel on top of the tree. Everyone tried reaching Violet, but no one could hold on. This time, he silently vowed, he'd grab her and never let go.

Seth took one ornament after another and hooked them on the tree alongside his grandmother. She hummed carols as they worked. He paused, holding a gingerbread man mid-air. "Is the church still going caroling tomorrow night?"

"Your mother said I would find you here."

Violet glanced up from her hunched position in front of an elderly woman. Her heart skipped a beat. His words from their dismissal meeting in her kitchen still rang in her mind: *Those weren't the plans God has for you.* Seth's words frightened her.

It didn't help that he looked at her like she was the next best thing to ice cream on a hot summer day, either. He grinned like a Basset Hound, lopsided and goofy.

She nearly smeared foundation down Ethel's neck.

The older woman sat, leaned back in a chair, with her eyes closed. Violet's hand twitched, poised over the woman's cheek, holding a small sponge of foundation. She swallowed hard, forced her gaze to drop, and resumed her task.

"It's no big secret." Violet tossed the sponge in a trash can nearby and dug into a bag on the counter beside her. "I come here once, sometimes twice a month to help out. Isn't that right, Ethel?"

Ethel smiled, peeking over at Seth, who stood beside her. "That's right. Takes ten years off us in one day."

"Twenty, if you ask me." Seth winked, and Ethel blushed.

Violet looked away as she pulled lip gloss from her bag and dabbed it on Ethel's puckered lips. She and her mother always volunteered, providing meals, crafts, and sometimes organizing trips. Now they came on separate days and different events.

In a lot of ways, Violet felt as if she could relate to the older ladies who came to the center. Many of them were widowed, some didn't have any children, and a few had never been married. Their aged wisdom brought comfort to her, especially on cold lonely days like these.

"Okay, Ethel, you're good to go." Violet put her cosmetics away.

"Thank you, dear," Ethel said as Seth reached to help her out of the chair. She walked across the room to a table full of seniors playing checkers, patting her hair, and smacking her lips together.

"All that for a game of checkers," Seth said.

"It's more than that," Violet explained. "It makes them feel special, they aren't given many excuses to get beautified these days, and when I come, it's like Christmas, and you'd think they were little girls again anxiously awaiting their turn."

Kyle's Aunt Joan started this ritual when crafts were repetitive, and games grew tiring for some. With the holiday approaching, Aunt Joan would say, "Violet, why don't you use your talents, honey, and give us old gals a trip to the spa, we've been everywhere else." And she had and kept on doing it for several years now.

According to the director of the center, more ladies showed up on the days she came then other days, even in the worst of weather.

Her gaze found his, staring at her intently. Heat rose in her cheeks.

"Something's come up about the house?" She asked with a heavy heart.

"Does it always have to be about the house? Or can I come as a friend?"

"I thought I tossed you out." She crossed her arms.

He shook his head. "You can't get rid of me that easy. I came to invite you to go caroling with me this evening. Would you like to go?"

She tilted her head and thought about his request. She hadn't gone caroling in years. Her heart hammered with the decision.

"Now, is that any way to ask out the young lady," a hunched old man said from behind her.

"You mean there's a better way?" Seth's eyes widened.

"You got to take her by the hand, look her straight in the eyes, and then pop the question."

Violet's throat constricted. She reached back and patted the older man on the shoulder. "Oh Mr. Rudrick, he's not asking me to marry him," But even as she said it, a lump formed in her throat. She blinked away the sudden moisture that blurred her vision.

Mr. Rudrick harrumphed. He waved his hand while grumbling, "Young folk today," as he staggered off with the use of his cane.

"Now where were we … Oh yes, I believe he said to take your hand and look you in the eyes." As he said it, he reached down, took her hand in his and looked into her eyes. She diverted her gaze and glanced around the center. His thumb brushed back and forth over the top of her hand. Her breath hitched in her throat, her gaze flew up to his face, and for a second, she almost let herself believe something more unique than friendship lingered between them.

She snatched her hand away. "I can't."

"Don't think of it as a date, Violet."

Her chest felt heavy. "It's not that, it's just …" This new feeling coming alive inside her … it frightened her.

"If it makes you feel better, it's a large group of people from our church. We get together and sing Christmas carols through the neighborhood. I'm just inviting you to come along. My grandmother and I go every year."

She groaned inwardly, Elaine would be there too.

"We'll grab something hot to drink and a few cookies afterward."

"Well, if you put it like that," She forced herself to smile, "There's just one thing I need to do before we leave."

"What's that?" he asked.

She held up a pair of clippers. "Give you a haircut."

They parked in the church parking lot, and Violet sat in the passenger seat of Seth's SUV. The evening grew dark, and under the lamplight, she could see the swirls of snow race across the church steps as the wind blew.

She sat and stared at the shadows of people standing inside the glass doors of the church.

"Ready?"

This morning she'd woken up and wound her clock. Now she pushed past the dread and waded through her fear to go caroling with a man who made her feel like a bowl of Jell-O.

"Why don't you go ahead in, I'll join you in a few minutes." She glanced at him, half expecting him to deny her request.

"Sure." He reached over and touched her arm. "Take your time, we're early." He slid out of the vehicle and left her alone. She watched as another car's headlights illuminated his form in the darkness as he walked to the brightly lit entrance of the church. She sank back into her seat.

When was the last time she'd entered this church, Easter? She never came on Christmas, not even with her mother.

Melancholy seeped through her veins, and she longed for what she would never have. She saw white velvet and dark red poinsettias but shook her head. Not to be so, God had a different plan for her. Seth had said so. They all did her mother, Nathan. She chortled bitterly. Everyone had plans for her, but no one allowed her to make choices of her own.

"Delight yourself in the Lord, and he will give the desires of your heart." She whispered the line of scripture from Psalms that had always been her favorite. Remembering the words shocked her. After all this time, she could still recall them. But, the desires of her heart were gone now. Her aspirations to be a wife and have a family of her own were buried alongside him on that fretful day of November. Or had they?

What plans do you have for me, Lord?

"I think we're ready to go now." Seth opened her door and handed her a fur muff. "This will help keep your hands warm, and I've got a wool cloak for you to wrap around yourself too."

Startled, she stared at him. The interior light highlighted his facial features and his expectant gaze. She took the muff and slid out of his vehicle. He reached around her and wrapped the cloak as she slipped her hands into the muff.

"Ready now?" he asked, wrapping his arm around her shoulder. She leaned into him as they walked, and he slid his arm around her waist. Outside the front steps, they gathered in a large group led by Pastor Lawrence and his wife.

At the first home, Pastor Lawrence knocked on the door. An older couple appeared in the threshold to watch from their doorstep. The group huddled together and sang.

"You know, *Oh, Holy Night,* right?" Seth teased before his tenor voice joined the others. Violet knew the words, but could not bring herself to sing. Seth's arm remained around her shoulders. Her voice felt as frozen as the icicles hanging from the older couple's rooftop.

At the fourth house, Violet's throat felt less constricted, and she found she could sing. Soft at first, but the words were audible. Seth smiled at her, and its warmth spread down to her toes. She spied a lit-up tree in the window of a house next door. Children stood in doorways with parents listening to them sing. They split a sugar cookie at the next house.

She spotted her mother and Mary Lou Jones towards the front of the group as they marched to the next house, but she didn't care. Walking down the sidewalks, her cheeks flushed with the cold, singing from house to house exhilarated her. She laughed at Pastor Lawrence's drawn-out antics to get through the snow of a home where the sidewalk hadn't been cleared. Slowly, she and Seth migrated into the center of the group.

Their caroling came to an end at the Lawrence's home, where they were invited in for hot chocolate, eggnog, and cookies. They shed their cloaks, and a woman stacked their fur muffs in a box for the next year.

Violet stood near the bay window in the living room, where Mrs. Lawrence had set out a nativity scene. She brushed her hand across the face of baby Jesus molded from porcelain.

"Christmas has always been a special time for me." Seth

handed her a cup of eggnog. "You have the lights, the tree, the presents, but then you have this baby who was God's gift to all of us."

"What God gives us, he takes away." Violet murmured. "Even Jesus was taken away."

Seth sipped his eggnog. "Jesus died upon the cross to bring us new beginnings in a fresh season of our life where he made us anew."

She turned, searched his face, and wished her faith could be as strong as Seth's. Gazing down at the baby Jesus, she thought about Gloria and the baby waiting to be born. Loss, her loss, of things she'd dreamed of caused an ache to throb in her chest. But as she gazed into Seth's compassion filled eyes, she didn't feel so lonely anymore. But would God take that away from her, too?

Seth had been appointed to sell her home, not fill her heart.

But, she could no longer deny that he had resided there, and the feelings she felt toward him brought a mixed combination of fear and joy.

When had it happened? When had she fallen in love with Seth? Realization jolted her, like static shock.

She was in love with Seth Jones!

"Violet?" he asked. His brows furrowed. She searched inside herself for something to say. Love, she decided, was fragile and easily stolen from one's heart.

"You've never had anything taken away like I have. You don't know what it's like. One day you're happy and about to be married, and then the next day you're attending a funeral instead of your wedding."

"Her name was Myra, and we weren't yet engaged, but I'd bought the ring and planned a romantic dinner for two. She never showed up. Just like my mother when I was seven, who left me with my grandparents on the night before Christmas. She never returned."

"I didn't realize."

"There are a lot of things you don't realize," Seth said, his voice wistful. "Life happens, just like my mother happened. Just like Myra happened. But God took those bad situations I was in and gave me better ones. My mother would have never been able to care for me the way my grandparents did or raise me the way they did. And obviously, God had someone else in mind for me than Myra. Although at the time, it didn't feel that way."

She heard the pain in his voice, the bitterness on his tongue, and she listened. Other people from their caroling group hung out in the kitchen in little corners conversing. She spotted Anne and Pete with their three boys talking to one of the Evans boys as they stood there in front of the nativity scene, secluded.

It felt like forever since she'd spent time amongst the people in this town. If not for Kyle's aunty Joan and that big house she lived in, Nathan and Kyle might not have met and her summers might have taken a different direction. And she cherished those summers the most. She hadn't realized how closed off she became after his death. She missed this. Missed him. But being here with Seth, put a salve over the ache and she focused on that.

"Your mother's still alive?"

Seth shrugged, took a sip of his drink. "I pray she'll come back home one day. Every year I hang a special bulb on the tree for her that I made that first Christmas. But I know she is in God's hands."

Sadness crept into her, and she felt a new ache form in her chest.

"And this, Myra? Did you ever see her again?"

"No, I'm sure it was better for both of us that we didn't."

Pastor Lawrence walked up beside Seth, touched his arm, and they shook hands. "Blustery night, but God's love be spread," he said.

"Felt like I was losing my voice there towards the end," Seth said.

"I believe we all were." Pastor Lawrence turned to Violet. His eyes grew sympathetic beyond the reaches of his smile. She attempted to smile back.

He held out his arms, and she found herself pulled into his embrace. "I'm so glad you could join us tonight." He patted her back.

"T-thank you," she stammered as he released her.

Pastor Lawrence looked between them, touched Seth on the shoulder, pointed above them, and moved on to the next group of people.

She and Seth both looked up at the same time. Above where Violet stood, hung mistletoe. Seth grinned.

Her tongue darted out and licked her bottom lip as she gazed around him to the others in the room.

"It would seem, my dear, you picked a good spot to stand this evening." He took her hand. "May I have the honor?"

Kissed by Seth? She found it hard to take a breath. Her insides squeezed closer together as her gaze darted around once more. She stepped back, but Seth stepped forward.

Her breath caught as he raised her hand to his lips and pressed them firmly to the top of her hand.

She stared at him, her jaw going slack, and her heart skipping a beat. He leaned forward, his breath warm on her cheek, and kissed her. Leaning back, he released her hand, and she placed it over her kissed cheek.

Blushing, she turned away so he couldn't see her smile, like a love-sick teenager.

Her heart swelled as fear trickled down her spine. How would she ever be able to keep Kyle alive in her heart while being in love with Seth?

11

A few days later, Seth appeared at Violet's door. She answered after the third knock with an apron tied around her waist, and her cheeks flushed.

"What's this, an olive branch?" she asked, opening the door.

"Actually, it's pine." He handed her the prickly branch as he slid his sunglasses atop his head and shook the snow from his boots.

"Thanks," she smelled it. "It's perfect for making face scrubs. You saved me a trip this week."

"You're kidding, right?" He followed her into the kitchen, a pot boiled on the stove, and several containers sat on the countertop. Smells of vanilla and peppermint enticed his nose. He found it more pleasant walking into these scents than those he'd been used to in the past month.

"Oh, these are perfect," she went on, saying, "I'll just chop up the needles and add some other exfoliates, and I'll whip up some of these before Christmas." She grinned at him. Somehow, he didn't think this was a joke.

"I can see now why you don't have a Christmas tree." He leaned against the counter, watching her pull off the needles and placing them into a bowl. She paused, put down the branch, and frowned.

Reaching over to stir the pot on the stove, she said, "I haven't put up a Christmas tree in years. This year doesn't seem to make any more sense than the others."

"Why this year?"

"Because if you and everyone else have their way, I'll just have to tear it down before Christmas." Her eyes watered, and she took a deep breath.

"Nothing lasts forever." Seth stepped close to her. She turned and bumped into him. He took her by the shoulders.

"I tell you what, I'll help you here. Then we'll go pick out a tree—just a small one. Then, when you move, you can take it with you."

"When are you going to understand, Christmas isn't the best time of year for me."

Seth raked his hands through his hair. There had to be a way to convince her to move on, help her find her place back in a faith-filled community, and open her heart that she may one day find a place inside it for him.

He thought then of the first time, he'd run into Violet, *"If you know what's good for you ... "*

"Your wedding day." Pieces of the puzzle started to fit together.

"Nice day to have a baby shower, right?"

"That's got to be rough." He didn't know why he'd brought that up.

Violet shrugged.

"I'm sorry, Violet. I can't let you drown yourself in your sorrows over the past."

"I learned to swim on my own a long time ago without anyone's help, thank you. I don't need anyone or anything to make me happy." That couldn't be further from the truth. Pain etched across her face. He reached out to touch her shoulder, and then he dropped his hand.

"Would it really be that bad to rely on someone else for once?"

Violet took the pot from the burner and turned off the stove. He heard her deep sigh. "You want to go get a tree, fine, but we've got to finish mixing up these lotions first. Then we'll go, and it better be a small tree, nothing too big. I can't handle that many needles at once."

"One Charlie Brown coming up."

A few hours later, Seth drove her south of town to a local tree farm where several cuts of pine leaned inside an old barn shed. Several acres around the farm's homestead were planted with blue spruce, evergreen, and various pine trees.

Patrons roamed the fields with axes over their shoulders. Inside the shed, the crisp scents of pine engulfed her. Seth wrapped his arm around her shoulder as they walked along the line of cut trees.

"Help you, folks?" A man walked up behind them, his jaw covered with a thick white beard. From beneath an orange toboggan cap, tufts of white hair stuck out.

They turned, and the Sam grinned. "Well, I'll be, how you doin', man?" Seth's eyes grew wide. The man stuck his hand out, and Seth shook it.

"The last place I'd thought to run into you," Seth said, shaking hands.

"Been sober now for over a year. The owner, Rob, came into the community center, needed some workers, and Dan over at the counseling center, done got me a job. Here I am."

"That's great, Joe." Seth stepped away from Violet and patted him on the shoulder. When he stepped back, she noticed the strain on his face.

"Seth seems to think I need a tree," she said.

"Well then, Miss, you've come to the right place, we got

trees. Just pick one out and let me know when you're ready to have it tied," Joe said.

Down the row, a man motioned he'd found his tree, and Joe walked away from them.

"Do you know that man?" she asked.

Seth looked at her a second—what felt like a minute—and answered her. "A long time ago." He wrapped his arm around her shoulder and turned his gaze away.

"Really? How?" She stepped over, inspecting a tree.

"My grandfather died my freshman year in college. It was the same year I met Myra. When she never showed for our dinner engagement, I called her. Another man answered the phone, she was in the background laughing, and I was left holding the bottle. I drank it, and when the pains of my losses were still there, I sought another."

And there she had been, standing in her kitchen with the stench of alcohol all around them a few weeks back. Even beer shampoo would have been tempting to a man she assumed was now sober.

For several long moments, she studied him, mortified. She considered apologizing. How many times had she said she was sorry to this man? More than she'd ever said to anyone else, she was sure.

Like her, Seth wasn't looking for sympathy.

"How long have you been sober?"

"Almost eight years." He walked away from her to a line of trees on the far side of the shed, leaving her to stare at his back.

Without a word, she slipped her hands around his arm and leaned into him. He gave her a wistful smile. She glanced down the row of trees and back at him.

Silently she prayed. As her time of vacating the house drew near, she was going to need all the help she could get if she wanted to hold onto Seth and their friendship in the days to come.

~

"What do you think?"

Violet rolled her eyes. At this rate, her mother would have her in the mall until closing time. Violet waved her hand, "It looks just like the other one you held up a second ago."

Elaine turned the small christening gown around in her hands and stared at it. "This one has white ribbon cuffs, the other one has lace."

Violet hitched her handbag back over her shoulder. "Does it matter?"

"I can't have my first grandson wearing something with frills and lace." Elaine picked up another, and Violet ran her hand down the silky texture of a gown hanging beside her.

"How do you know it's not a girl?" she asked, and Elaine paused.

"I just know. After you've been a mother, as I have, you recognize those types of things." Elaine picked out another gown. "What about this one?"

"Why don't you just give the baby Nathan's?"

"I thought of that, but the bonnet is missing." Elaine held out the gown for her own inspection.

Violet walked past her mother to a rack of white bonnets and sorted through them. "Here, it's white."

Her mother took the bonnet. "I realize this must be hard for you."

Hard wasn't the word. She handed the bonnet to her mother. "I'll meet you at the deli two stores down when you're finished."

She walked out of the store and into the Lexington mall, where crowds of people flocked up and down the hall between storefronts. Above the noise of people, came the cheerful holiday music that made her feel nauseous. It was more than missing a meal; it was the countdown of days that disturbed her.

McPhee's was packed for lunch. She slid into a corner booth where her mother could spot her easily enough in her bright red turtle neck sweater. From across the deli, Violet spied a tall gentleman wearing a NASCAR jacket with the number six on the back. She shook her head to clear her vision, but when she looked again, he was still there. Beside him, digging in a small leopard print purse, was Kyle's mother.

There was no mistake. Violet picked up a menu, hoping to shield herself from view, but it was too late. She heard the high-pitched squeal of Miranda Freeman as the couple walked towards her.

"Look, there's Violet!"

Violet peered around the menu. Suddenly, she felt ill and laid it down, "We've wanted to stop by and see you." Miranda walked over to Violet's booth. Robert and Miranda Freeman were the last people on her shopping list this year, and God forgive her. The only thing she intended to give them was big fat lump of coal.

"I'm sure you have." Violet folded her hands in front of her.

Robert and Miranda looked at each other as if neither knew what to say next. Violet had no intention of inviting them to join her. She checked her watch, wondering what was taking her mother so long.

"We're sorry about the house, honey," Miranda said, scooting into the booth on the other side of Violet. Robert stood at her side.

The past year since the first letters from the attorney had arrived filled her with bitterness. These two people had been like family to her, would have been family to her. When her dad had passed away, Robert Freeman took Nathan and her under his wing as one of his own. Until that fretful day, they'd all walked out of the hospital, except Kyle.

She fought to reign in her hatred for these people. Part of

her forgave them, but the other part, the part that couldn't ever forget the way they treated her at Kyle's funeral, still harbored those pent-up feelings.

Now, the woman had the nerve to apologize.

"You know we feel awful about what's happened in the past." Miranda went on. "We've been thinking …" Miranda looked up at her husband.

Violet arched a brow. She wasn't about to make this easy on them.

"You've gotten settled in the house now, and it isn't fair to have to make you move. The only reason we wanted to sell it was so we could build another car and get back to racing, and go on with our lives. It's not the same, not without …"

"Kyle's car." There she said it. Miranda's eyes grew wide. Robert half smiled and placed his hand on Miranda's shoulder.

Miranda's eyes glistened as her husband spoke. "We built that car with our own two hands, my boys and me. Like you, we just want something to hold on to and remember him by."

"It was never his car to give you in the first place." Miranda's voice crackled.

They had almost had her fooled, for a second she would have believed them, but Miranda's voice made her wince like nails on a chalkboard.

"What do I get?" Violet asked. Her body trembled as the bitter sludge seeped out of her heart, and all the hatred, anger, and hurt flowed into her veins.

"You can have the house, just like you've always wanted." Miranda's gaze sought Robert's with triumph. "We'll have the attorney draw up the papers. This will be the best gift for Scott."

Violet gripped the table. It took every ounce of her control to hold her composure. Her head threatened to spin. "You can do that? The house is already sold."

"Not if we don't sign the papers. We can back out of the

sale, there's still time, and have the documents processed in your name," Robert said.

"You title us the car, and we'll give you the full deed to the house." Miranda grinned. Her plum lips the same shade as her blush. The woman never did listen to any of Violet's advice.

"I don't want the house, not anymore." Hadn't that been what she always wanted? These past few weeks, she'd mourned. At night, she'd dreamed her lonely dream of loss and regrets, full of sorrow. In the days, she'd walked around the house, touched the curtain in the kitchen window, caressed the bathroom faucet, and laid her cheek against the walls of her bedroom. All places Kyle had mended in preparation of them living together as man and wife.

Miranda sat back, dumbfounded. "What do you mean you don't want it anymore?"

Violet took a deep breath to settle her insides from quivering. "Just as I said, I don't want it anymore. I've found a new home. I'll be moving on the same day we sign the papers for the house."

Miranda slapped her palms on the table. "And the car?"

"How much?" Robert interrupted. "Name your price."

Violet looked at them, both their faces washed in desperation. Behind them, a waitress walked up, paused, and put her finger up that she'd be back in a minute. Violet spotted her mother entering the establishment and smiled. An uplifting sense of peace washed over her.

"You can't have it."

Robert Freeman's face turned so red, she feared it would blister. Miranda jerked herself out of the booth. "Why you …"

Elaine walked up behind them. "Robert, Miranda, out shopping?" She asked in a most pleasant voice.

Miranda's mouth clamped shut. She gazed around as the patrons of McPhee's grew quiet. Glaring at Violet with dark penetrating eyes, Miranda dragged her husband out of the establishment by the arm.

"Have I become like them?"

Elaine gave her that look, and Violet held up her hand. "You know what, you don't need to answer that."

12

She heard the knock, and the sound of the front door opening. He slipped off his jacket and walked into the dining room.

She lifted her gaze, her eyes pinned him in motion. The sheer emotion in his stare caused her heart to jolt.

She stood at the dining room table, clipping bottle labels and tying them onto her finished product with a ribbon.

"You're upset."

"I hate to be rude, but if you could show yourself out the same way you let yourself in, that would be great." *Before I fall to pieces.*

She'd been mixing up shampoo, experimenting with a new flavor of lip gloss, and whipping up facial creams for days. But the scene of running into Kyle's parents at the mall had kept replaying in her memory.

"Is there anything I can do?" When she looked at him, it was a different man she saw. The hair was darker, the eyes blue. The ridge of his nose more slanted with a small bump from being broken once too often.

Violet blinked.

It had been a long time since she'd been this way. Several

different emotions raged inside her, tugging her in different directions at the same time.

Violet covered her eyes with her hands. The dull thud of a migraine hammered on her head. "No, please just go."

He didn't move. Violet refused to look up into his face again. She felt his gentle touch at her elbow, and she jerked it back. Her eyes clashed with brown ones. They drew her into their depths like a warm blanket on a cold day.

They were brown, not blue. Even though Violet buzzed his thick curls of hair away with her clippers, she felt more attracted to him. Or perhaps, she thought, it was the exhaustion catching up to her.

Violet stood and stared at him.

Seth held on to her, afraid she'd faint. Her pale complexion went ghostly white. The way she looked at him now haunted his heart. There was blankness in her gaze like she looked right at him and couldn't see him. Her eyes grew large. She fluttered those long thick lashes repeatedly as if to clear her vision.

"I didn't see you in church this morning."

"I'm sorry," she stammered. "I'm not feeling well."

"I can see that." He pulled out a chair and offered her a seat. Violet shook her head, but the rattle inside made her ill. "When is the last time you had a decent meal?" She had the dimensions of a maple sapling.

"I'm not hungry," she sat, covering her face in her hands. Seth felt his brows draw together. He left her to investigate inside the refrigerator.

"I expected as much." He looked at the meager contents of her stock. A cup of half-eaten yogurt, hard moldy cheese, and a half-gallon of milk that made his stomach roll over. He turned back to her in the dining room. "Do you like Italian? Or I know a really great Mexican place over near Hatton"

"I'm not going out."

"Great, Italian, it is." He pulled out his cell phone. He ordered a large pizza, salad, and drinks as she peered at him through spread fingers. "Twenty minutes." He placed the phone back at his hip. "Now, what can I get you in the meantime?"

"Aspirin," she said.

The food arrived over twenty minutes later. Violet's head had stopped pounding. The hammer had gotten tired of striking her sensitive nerves.

Seth rummaged through her drawers for flatware. The aroma of the pizza he sat in front of her made her stomach growl, and her cheeks grew hot. He didn't seem to notice while he poured them each a glass of soda.

Violet bit into the first warm slice, careful of the running cheese. She devoured one slice, then two. Seth pushed a salad toward her. An amused expression softened the features of his face.

"I'm glad you weren't hungry. I'd say it was more like famished." He bit into his slice of pizza. At this rate, she'd finish half the pizza without Seth taking his first bite. She didn't know what had gotten into her. Seth would think she was some kind of a glutton the way she stuffed her face.

Violet leaned away from the table. There were only two pieces left. She sipped her soda, looking down at the empty dishes.

Seth laughed. The deep, rich, smooth kind of laugh she'd longed to hear once more. "What?" She couldn't stop grinning. "Alright, maybe I was hungry," she said. "A little." She indicated with her fingers.

His mouth cracked a half-amused smile. "If that's a little, then I wonder what a lot would be. I don't think I've ever met anyone who ate more than me that was female." He laughed.

Violet laughed, too.

"Last piece?" He held it out for her. She couldn't remember the last time when she'd done more than pick at a meal." She *had* been starving!

"I'm stuffed." She patted her stomach. After a meal like that, she was bound to sleep all night.

"Good," He cleared away the plates.

"I'll take care of that." She rose to meet him at the sink. "Really, just leave them."

"Are you sure?" he asked.

"Yes," she picked up the empty pizza box and set it near the recycling bin. When she turned, she found Seth a hair's breadth away. A flutter teetered in her stomach. His arms wrapped around her and drew her into his embrace, and her pulse sped.

Slowly, his head bent towards her. She looked away, afraid that her emotions might be written in her expression. Seth held onto her tightly. She felt his warm lips touch her temple, and she rested her head on his shoulder.

"Long day?" he asked.

"Let's just say it's been a long week." She closed her eyes, allowing herself to absorb the warmth of his embrace.

"Is the holiday season like this every year?"

Seth had a way of making her feel … soft. Aware of the gentler side that she oftentimes tried to hide.

She hadn't seen him in nearly a week. She should have returned his phone calls or dropped by his office, but the harder she tried not to think of him, the more he entered her thoughts.

Nearly two months ago, she wouldn't have let Seth Jones anywhere near her. Regardless of her resistance, his consistent antics had brought him into her life. Despite knowing what was good for him. In the blink of an eye, he could go tomorrow. Grief washed over her.

She couldn't allow Seth to come any nearer. If loving him meant they must remain apart, then she would be willing to sacrifice their friendship.

God knew she wasn't any good for him.

Seth brushed his knuckles down her cheek. She placed her hand over his. He bent towards her, and she sprang back out of his hold. Her heart beating rapidly.

Before he could react, Violet reached for the first thing her hand came in contact with—a broom. "Unless you want …" she threatened, looking over at the broom in her hand. "Unless you want a broom over your head, I suggest you leave!"

He held up his hands, "I'm harmless."

She shook her head and held up the broom in a warning. Harmless, she laughed, harmless indeed. *Please, Lord, let this be the right thing to do.* She let out a long breath as she watched him back out of the kitchen. She followed him through the dining room and watched as he slipped on his jacket and buttoned it.

"I promise I won't try to kiss you," he said.

"Nope, not good enough. I need you to leave."

He chuckled. "My hands in my pockets?"

"Out. I want you gone."

His expression sobered. He shook his head. A few moments later, she heard his footsteps, and then the front door bang shut.

To ease her frustration, she swept up the mess on the dining room floor.

The night brought dark circles to her eyes. A red splotch on her cheek would be acne before the day was out. Violet pulled on an old cotton shirt and faded jeans. The weather called for another six to eight inches of snow with a wind chill below zero.

Last week, it had been nearly forty; December was turning out to be one of the coldest seasons she remembered.

"Violet, it's your mother. Pick up."

Reaching back and pulling her hair into a ponytail, she picked up the phone. Before she could say hello, her mother was talking. "Gloria's at the hospital, she's dilated, but there hasn't been any progress all night."

All night? Gloria went to the hospital sometime yesterday? She slumped into a nearby chair and hung her head. Whatever Violet had wished upon her brother and Gloria before this had evaporated. Now she silently prayed as her mother continued with details about Gloria's hospitalization.

Lord, if you've ever heard any of my prayers, please listen to me now. Forgive me. I'm sorry. Let Gloria and the baby be alright—for Nathan's sake. I'll even let Seth back into my life if that is your plan for me.

As her mother concluded, Violet picked up the phone. "Call me if anything changes."

Suddenly, her problems didn't seem so important anymore.

She sank her face into her hands and wept.

This time it was fear that enveloped her. Gut-wrenching cries arose from within her. This couldn't be happening again. Not Gloria, not the baby. Poor Nathan.

"I didn't mean it," she whispered. Memories of her life before Kyle's death flashed in her mind, all the times she'd shunned Gloria, and *oh Lord forgive her*, how many times had she refuted that innocent child? She didn't mean it.

Her thoughts turned to the Freemans, and her heart lurked in pain. Everyone wanted something from her, but she had nothing left to give, not life itself was hers anymore. Yet, she'd gladly give it at this moment if it meant Gloria's baby would live.

Her mother hadn't said so, but the strain and the worry in her tone of voice lead Violet to believe that Gloria and the baby were in trouble.

"This is all my fault," she said.

Newspaper articles and nightly news presses echoed in her ears. *Bride Attends Funeral on her Wedding Day, Widowed Without A Ring, The Last Lap* ...

She clutched her hands over her ears to block out the sounds in her head. Details of Kyle's accident evaded her. It was an accident, pure and simple. It wasn't Nathan's fault, but she'd blamed him. So much so, that she'd caused him to question his faith, which had led him on the path where Gloria had found him.

She had been just as lost, just as hurt, and just as yearning as he was, but no one had found her. Or had they? She thought of Seth and felt a part of her ache ease.

It had been such a long time since she'd prayed, a real heartfelt prayer, the words were hard at first, but like always, she cut to the point. "Please don't let anything happen to Gloria and the baby. This is my fault." She felt fresh tears run down her face. "I let him go, I trusted you to bring him back!" she was yelling now, her voice hollow in the room. "Why? Why didn't you bring him back?"

She'd always been taught to believe God had a reason for everything. Why did she have to be alone when Nathan was not? Why did Seth have to be the one to sell her house? The anguish of the past scarred her, and she'd turned away from those she'd loved.

"I want to go home." She gulped, squeezing her eyes shut. How could she, after all, she'd done?

"If you want to punish me, go ahead. You can't hurt me anymore. Kyle, this house, what next? Gloria? The baby?"

The faint sounds of a snowplow moving down the street answered her.

Had God even heard her cry?

For he will never leave you nor forsake you, drifted into her thoughts. She wiped the tears dry on her cheeks and bowed her head. She found herself exhausted, clutching herself, and crumbling to the floor.

With a deep breath, she released the final sorrows of her heart as she lay on the tattered carpet in the middle of the room. "Lord, forgive me."

13

Seth picked up the phone, hung it up, paused, and then picked it back up again. Eventually, Violet would have to return his call. He looked at the clock. He'd promised Tracy he'd stay until closing. Yet, Violet hadn't answered her phone all day. As he got up and reached for his jacket, Tracy walked in and leaned against the doorway.

"Going somewhere?"

"What's up?" Seth shrugged into his jacket and looked over his shoulder.

"Freeman's attorney called. They're backing out of the sale."

Seth paused mid-reach through his second coat sleeve. "They can't," he said, knowing that they very well could.

"I don't know." Tracy slapped the folder on his desk. "It's your deal, you take care of it."

Seth reached over, picked up the folder, and opened it. He winced, flipping through the pages and reached for the phone as it shrilled on his desk.

"Smith and Jones Realty."

～

She sat, with her arms across the steering wheel, her head resting on top of them, inside the driver's seat of Kyle's stock car.

The garage was flooded with the bright lights of the fluorescent bulbs overhead and the sunlight pouring through the open door. It smelled like burnt oil and mixed gasoline. Yet, the leather upon the steering wheel still bore the imprints where Kyle's fingers had once gripped.

She rested her cheek upon those prints and sighed. There wasn't an inch of this car that he hadn't touched. Under the hood lay remnants of nicked knuckles and sweaty palms piercing the engine to bring life to pressed metal and wheels.

She heard the hum, the roar, the idling of the cars zooming down the track taking curve after curve around the speedway.

"I've been looking all over for you."

Violet looked over, she hadn't heard him approach. Seth crouched near the driver side door, he reached and pulled the belted netting back from the window and peered in.

"You've talked to Elaine?" Violet lifted her head from the wheel.

"She called me a little while ago, seems she's been trying to get hold of you all day. She was worried."

Violet hadn't thought about anyone trying to get hold of her. After she'd been able to pull herself off the floor, she'd come here and lost track of time.

"Gloria and the baby?"

"They're doing just fine. The baby was born a few hours ago."

As if there had been a restraint on her lungs, she felt it release, and she sighed. She looked over at Seth and felt herself smile. His hair was a mess, and little lines of stress stretched from around his mouth. If she didn't know better, she would have thought he was worried about her, too.

She reached over and brushed a dark lock of hair from his forehead.

"It's a real beauty." He clamped his hand on the window opening. "I don't believe I ever saw him race this one."

She pulled her hand back, felt her cheeks grow hot. "This was the first car he ever raced, it was his first victory before all the sponsorships started taking over." She rested her chin back down, looking into his soft brown eyes.

"I can see why he would hold on to it. You never forget your first."

"He built this car from the frame up." She could understand the Freeman's sentiments about it, the labor they'd induced to build it, and the reason they'd want it back now that Kyle wouldn't ever be driving it again.

"I saw him race a couple of times. He's not someone you easily dismiss."

She nodded, reaching up to the top of the window and climbing out of the car. Seth stood and grasped her by the waist, lifting her out. As he set her back down on her feet, he kept hold of her in his embrace.

"How did it happen?"

For a moment, she considered whether to answer him or not. Nobody had asked her that question before, most everyone knew. Perhaps he was being polite to inquire, she mulled leaning back against the car

"It was Nathan's idea." Maybe that's why it hurt so much. "My brother, the daredevil, couldn't have a bachelor party like other guys. They had to go do something exciting and dangerous."

Seth was quiet, watching her as she recounted that awful day in her past.

"I don't know what's worse, hearing the doctor tell us Kyle was dead or standing inside the church attending a funeral on what should have been my wedding day."

He reached over and gave her hand a squeeze.

"I haven't been to church since." She took a deep breath. "The day I ran into you at Gloria's baby shower, all I could think about was my wedding shower, people standing in the pews of the church on my wedding day, and watching Kyle from the front of the church in a casket. I didn't want to be there, I couldn't ..."

"It's no wonder." He pulled her close.

"I feel like I've been on a roller coaster for a very long time, and I've finally come to an end where it's time to step off, but because I've been riding for so long, I don't know how to get out of my seat."

"Life is full of unexpected twists and turns, things we can't change or explain. The reasons withheld from us by the one who gave us this life." Seth cupped the side of her face, and her hand reached up to cover his.

"I'm sorry. When you came the other day, I was upset, but not at you. It was the Freeman's. They'd cornered me a few days ago."

"About the house, right?"

She stepped back from him, "How did you know?"

"What did they want?"

She reached over and ran her hand across the hood of the car.

"Just promise me the next time you step into a roller coaster that you'll take me along for the ride?"

She saw a flicker in his eyes and nodded at him.

"I would have come sooner, but I had some things I had to clear up."

She stepped back from him, "It's about the house, isn't it?"

"I'm afraid so."

"What happened?"

You, walking into my life and making me feel this way.

∼

Violet walked down the chilled hallway of the maternity ward in the hospital. Seth had offered to come along, but she decided this was something she needed to do on her own.

She heard the low murmurs of voices in the rooms as she passed. The nurse's station was quiet. A nurse looked up and smiled at her as she passed. She waited for the electronic doors to open and went through.

She'd expected the sterile smells of antiseptics but instead was relieved by the faint scents of formula and baby powder that tickled her nose. She couldn't help pressing her face to the cool window to search for baby Harding.

A girl, Seth had told her. She had a niece. Violet lifted a silent thank you to God for the blessing of Gloria and Nathan's daughter. She had a long way to go in her walk, but her journey of faith was just beginning anew.

"Can I help you?" The nurse from the nurse's station inquired, peering in on the babies with Violet.

"I was just looking to see my niece." Violet said, feeling a sensation of joy swell in her chest. and a little disappointed that she could spot no babies with the name of 'Harding.'

"Most babies stay in the room with their mothers." The nurse, whose name badge said "Anne," informed Violet.

"Oh," Violet didn't know what room Gloria would be in, she hadn't thought to ask.

"Harding, right?"

"Yes," Violet said, amazed Anne would know.

"Room 230 down on your left. Mother hasn't let that baby out of her arms since she woke up."

"They are both fine?" Of course, they were, hadn't Seth said so?

Anne patted her on the arm. "They are doing wonderful. Cutest little thing I've seen in a long time." Another nurse strolled by adjusting a pair of teal scrubs and tucking another roll in her waistband. The bright blue shirt she wore was splattered with bright pink daisies.

Violet headed in the direction of Gloria's room. She hesitated just outside the doorway. Was this a part of what it felt like to come home?

Her hands trembled. From across the hall, she heard a baby cry.

Nathan sat on the edge of the bed, cooing at his daughter held in Gloria's arms. Violet glanced down at the gift she had brought for the new mother in her hand. Gloria probably didn't need any of it. Beneath it all, she had to be tired.

Quietly, Violet walked into the room, thinking of the item she'd picked up along the way to the hospital. "Something pink." She had told the clerk who offered her assistance. The package she'd carried out was neatly wrapped and tucked into her shoulder bag.

At first, the couple didn't notice her. They fawned over the sleeping babe between them. Violet felt her throat clog and cleared it. Nathan looked up. His expression turned from delightful to reserve in a heartbeat. Gloria smiled wanly at her.

"Violet," Gloria ran a hand down the delicate cheek of the baby nestled lovingly in her arm. "What a wonderful surprise."

"I wouldn't have thought you'd come here."

The devil himself was more welcomed than she, but Violet didn't hold it against them. She had that coming.

Gloria's free hand brushed Nathan's arm.

"Elaine called earlier."

"You just missed her." Nathan kept his hands near his daughter. "She and Noreen went to the house." Noreen, Violet knew, was Gloria's mother.

"I tried telling them not to bother," Gloria said.

"Let them nest. You've been doing it all week." Gently, Nathan pushed Gloria's rising form back into the pillows behind her. "Rest while you can."

"You had better listen to him. He can be quite stubborn."

Violet stood at the foot of the bed. The room seemed small, with the three of them and the baby. A television hung above them, running an old rerun of a sitcom, but the volume had been put on mute. The stand beside the window was busting with a variety of pink daisies and roses. A few baskets lined the window sill with fruit and gifts.

"Look who's talking." The jibe was light.

"I came here to apologize." There, she'd said it.

Gloria and Nathan looked at one another, then at Violet, the shocked expressions genuine on their faces. Violet didn't wait for a cue. "I was angry, and I've been taking it out on you. It's taken me all this time to come to terms with what happened, and I realize that there shouldn't be any blame on your part."

Gloria's hand squeezed Nathan's.

"I had a nice long talk with God, and I think I've gotten things straightened out now."

"Do you?" Nathan asked, his shoulders drew back.

"I don't know for sure, but I think it's a start, and that's all I'm asking you for ... a chance to start over." Violet gripped the straps of her shoulder bag, unconsciously holding her breath.

"There's no starting over, where there is no end," Nathan said.

"So, where do I go from here?" Violet half-whispered, half-croaked.

"Where ever your heart leads you." Nathan left his wife's bedside and stood in front of Violet. "Trust your heart." He laid his hand on her shoulder.

Her vision became blurred with the rim of tears in her lashes. "Can you forgive me?"

Nathan pulled her into a hug. "Welcome back, Twig, I've missed you." As fleeting as it appeared, it was gone. Gloria gasped as the baby smiled. "I guess this means she approves."

Nathan laughed.

Gloria held out an arm, and Violet embraced her too. The three of them sat on Gloria's bed, rehashing old times.

"I almost forgot." Violet reached into her bag. "I brought you something for the baby." She handed the gift to Nathan. Gloria motioned for him to open it. A small pink bonnet emerged from white tissue paper.

"Oh, Violet, It's adorable!" Gloria said.

"I have something for you too." Violet handed Gloria a bottle of orange blossom lotion.

"My favorite. Thank you for remembering."

A pair of blue eyes popped open.

"Look who decided to wake up!" Nathan lifted the small bundle from Gloria's arms. "Twig, meet your niece, Christine Faith Harding." Nathan placed the baby in Violet's arms. She looked down through the stream of tears at her niece.

"Hello there." Violet crooned. "I'm your Auntie Twig, and I promise I'll always spoil you."

14

On the next day, Violet slumped in a chair in Seth's office.

"I should have figured something like this would happen."

Concerns continued to disrupt her sleep, like what would happen now with the contract to buy the other house.

"I've put a call into the attorney. I'm sure since the Freeman's were able to flip the table on you and force you out, that we may be able to do the same to them."

That's precisely what the Freeman's wanted. If they couldn't have what they wanted, then neither could she. But now, she wasn't so sure exactly what she did want. Her house, Kyle's house, or any other, none of them had ever really seemed like home.

A home was a place that brought comfort and joy to one's heart.

"No," Violet said. She sighed and leaned forward, placing her hand on his arm. "Just let them have it."

Seth's brows drew together, and he stared at her for a long moment. Then a smile spread across his face. "You know what this means don't you?"

She hadn't really thought about it. She supposed she'd have to move in with her mother now. The other house would be a dream left unfulfilled, but at least the Freeman's wouldn't be able to use the house to try to blackmail her anymore.

Her heart ached for him. "You'll lose your commission on both sales. Won't you get anything?"

He placed his other hand atop hers. "Just the company of a good woman."

She felt her cheeks warm, looking down at his hands, bigger than hers, stronger. And, somehow, it felt right to hold on to him.

"It's Christmas Eve tomorrow, do you think you can arrange for the attorney to give the Freeman's the good news before the New Year?" Violet pondered their reaction, she didn't want to spoil their Christmas, although she already had by not giving them Kyle's car.

"I think I can arrange that, on one condition." Seth leaned forward. "Come to church with me tomorrow night."

There would be a service, and the church window sills would be lined with bright red poinsettias. She felt the palms of her hands grow slick with sweat.

"Violet." Seth's voice was soft, and she gazed into his eyes. Did he have any idea what he was asking her to do?

"I d-don't know if I can," she said.

"You won't be going in alone, not this time. I'll be right by your side."

"Promise?"

"Cross my heart." He swept his finger across his chest.

Violet scanned the parking lot for Seth's vehicle. They agreed to meet here. Seth called and said he had a few last-minute errands he had to run. She arrived early, she told herself. Seth still had plenty of time to get here before the services started.

It started snowing earlier in the day, little white specks clustering on her windshield as she sat inside her car waiting.

Beside her, a dark SUV pulled up, but Seth's was silver. That couldn't be him.

She waited.

She watched groups of people walk across the parking lot with their heads ducked against the wind. The Patterson's, the Myers, and old man Evans and one of his sons. How long had it been since she felt comfortable around any of them. Except maybe for Anne and maybe Gwen. But they all had families and lives and given up on calling or coming around a long time ago. It had been her fault. Ignoring them. Hiding in that house away from and trying to keep a hold of a dying dream and a ghost of a man.

An older woman held the door for another older woman. Sister, Violet decided, the two who spent time volunteering in the library. She done enough reading during sleepless nights after Kyle's accident to keep her from the pain of reality for far too long.

She pulled back her coat sleeve and checked the time, fifteen minutes before service started. Seth would be driving into the parking lot any second, just like clockwork.

She tapped her gloved tipped fingers on the steering wheel. One minute went by, then another. Her fingers curled around the steering wheel, any minute Seth would be here, she told herself. Any minute.

But as another minute went past, and she watched more vehicles pull into spaces, and heard car doors shut. Still no Seth. She recalled their conversation earlier in the day, it made her smile. He didn't mention anything about being late.

He wasn't late. She was just early.

Violet shivered and turned the heat up full blast. Soon car arrivals subsided, and she sat alone, surrounded by empty cars. She watched through the snow speckled windshield as the church doors opened and admitted church members and their families. She saw the shadows from the light inside fall across the cement stairs at the front of the church.

Where was Seth? He'd promised to be here.

She sucked in a sharp breath and covered her face with her hands. How could she have been so silly! Of course, Seth wasn't going to come driving into the parking lot, she laughed. He was already here! No wonder he wanted to meet her here, he was probably part of the service and had to come early.

She turned off the engine, gathered her purse, and got out of her car. She stood in the snow-covered parking lot and looked out towards the church. It had been snowing then too, she remembered, taking those first steps towards the front doors.

A brisk wind caught her in the face and pushed her back. She wrapped her arms around herself and ducked her head. At the bottom of the front steps of the church, she looked back. There was nothing behind her except a trail of her own footprints shining in the street lights.

She took a deep breath, climbed the stairs to the glass door, and from inside two teenage girls dressed in dark green velvet, smiled at her. Her hand wavered, reaching for the door handle.

Her heart seized, and her hand dropped to her side. She looked back, and a vision of men in dark suits marching up the stairs swept past her like the wind blowing harshly on her face. Deep-seated pain crippled her and twisted away, bent over.

The taller of the two teenage girls pushed opened the door and asked, "Are you alright?" The shorter girl peered around her.

Violet bit her lip and nodded.

"It's warmer inside," offered the other girl.

"I just need a minute." Violet tried to force a smile.

"Okay." The taller girl said, "You still have time yet before service starts." The two girls resumed their prior places at the welcoming center—watching and whispering occasionally.

Violet turned around and leaned back against the glass

doors. A few stragglers came past, and she stepped aside so they could enter the church. A few she recognized, and when they said hello, she tried harder to smile.

They, too, had been here on that fateful day for a funeral.

Another chill ran down her throat, despite the scarf she wore, and the wind pulled fiercely at her wool cap.

If Seth were inside, wouldn't he have been waiting for her at the door?

The sounds of a vehicle's tires crunching across the snow caught her attention, but what little hope had filled her disappeared as the outline of a truck came into view.

What was she thinking, agreeing to come here? She shook her head and was about to take a step off the landing onto a stair when she heard. "After you."

Violet looked up into the withered old face of Mr. Delcamp, hunched down and clutching to the support of his cane. As a child, Violet had thought the man old when he was her third grade teacher. Now she wondered if he would disappear into the woodwork and become a permanent part of the church one day.

"You go ahead," she said.

"Service is inside, Child." Mr. Delcamp shook his cane to ward off the snow and held the door open for her.

"Thank you, but I'm waiting for someone." She took hold of the door, relieving him of its pressing weight.

"Suit yourself." He wobbled inside. Violet held out her hand as if to catch him, afraid he would fall.

After the door closed, she watched him converse with the two teenage girls before hobbling down the hall to the sanctuary.

Looking back out across the parking lot, not a single space was left empty. The flow of people in the hallway had faded.

Where was Seth?

The cold bit at her legs beneath her long wool skirt. She walked down the stairs and paced in front of them. Perhaps he was in there, waiting for her to join him. Hadn't he known that she wouldn't be able to walk into the church alone? Didn't he say he'd be right beside her?

She climbed back up the stairs. One of the teenage girls opened the door again to speak to her. "They are going to be starting in a few minutes."

'Have you seen a tall gentleman, about six feet tall, with brown curly hair and brown eyes?"

"I think I know who you're talking about, but I haven't seen him." The girl shook her head. "You can go in and look, or if he comes, I'll tell him you're inside."

"Violet?" Elaine's voice rang in the front entrance of the church. "I can't believe you're here!" She saw the tears well up in her mother's eyes. "Where's Seth? Did he come with you?"

Elaine grasped the door. A red poinsettia pinned to the lapel of her suit jacket. "Goodness, you must be frozen standing out there, why don't you come inside?"

Violet didn't hear her "He's not here?"

Elaine frowned, tugging on Violet's arm until Violet found herself standing a few steps inside the doorway of the tall glass doors. "Not yet. Why don't you come in and sit with us? Nathan and Gloria are here with the baby, and Missy here can tell Seth to join us when he comes."

Violet gazed over at the young girl who bobbed her head in agreement. Elaine extended her hand to Violet.

Her heart slammed in her chest as she glimpsed down the hallway to the sanctuary and heard the first melody of organ music. She reached back and clamped hold of the door handle.

"I'm sorry, Mother. I can't." Not without Seth.

Elaine's eyes filled with tears. "We're in the fourth pew on the left-hand side." She sniffled. "Why don't I just wait here with you, and we'll go in together when you're ready."

Violet shook her head. Voices floated out of the sanctuary singing *O, Holy Night.*

"I'm sure he'll be here any moment, Violet. Mary Lou arrived early to practice with the choir."

Violet turned and rested her head against the cold glass door. Her hands gripped the door handle. There was no white paper runner for her to follow. Nor anyone's arm extended to escort her down the aisle.

She took a deep breath.

"When is the last time you spoke to him?"

"This morning." Violet pulled her handbag off her shoulder and rummaged around for her cell phone. No messages or missed calls.

"Perhaps you should try calling him," Elaine said.

Violet flipped open her phone and called Seth. She stood tapping her booted heel on the tile as she counted the rings. She heard the operator come on and hung up. He either didn't have his phone turned on or was in an area where he didn't get service. She tried his office number, but no one picked up. It was Christmas Eve.

She snapped her phone shut and tossed it back inside her bag.

"Where can he be?" She felt it, the same feeling she'd felt waiting at the hospital when she'd broken his nose. She felt her body tremble.

"I'm sure he is fine. He's just running a few minutes late."

"You don't understand. The man runs like a clock. Late isn't in his vocabulary." For weeks, Seth had been showing up to bring her lunch or take her out to dinner. In the middle of the day, he'd show up for no reason but to say hello.

He was there for her.

But where was he now?

She felt what little composure she had left crumbling. Where was he?

"Did you try his house phone?" Elaine asked.

"I don't have it," Violet said, trying not to roll her eyes. Not many people still had house phones these days.

Seth lived with his grandmother, and Mary Lou was here, by her mother's account.

"Why don't I go find Mary Lou, maybe she'll know where he might be," Elaine said.

"I don't want to worry her." Violet was filled with enough worry for the both of them. "Maybe I misunderstood him, and he's sitting at the house waiting to pick me up." She pushed on the door.

Elaine grabbed her by the arm. "You'd miss the whole service running home to check."

"You don't think he is there, do you?" Violet felt the pent up fears inside her unravel.

"No, I don't. Where ever Seth is, he'll be here, if he told you he'd meet you here, then I believe you have to trust that he'll get here. It may not be on our time, but the roads are getting slick with snow, and you would want him to be safe, right?"

"Of course." She should have known better than to fall in love with him.

Everything inside her went still. She stared at Elaine as if her own mother had been foreign to her until this moment. What if it was happening all over again?

She shook her head, *not*.

She loved him, and with that love, she understood what love meant. Sometimes one had to let go in order to embrace God's plan. No matter what that may be.

Elaine peered at her strangely.

"Please, Mother, just go inside. This is something I need to do on my own."

Elaine tilted her chin up, staring at Violet. "You care about him, don't you?"

Elaine walked up and embraced her.

"You wouldn't be so upset if you didn't. I'll go see what I can find out to ease your worries from Mary Lou, and I'll pray for you both."

"Thank you," Violet said.

Elaine stepped back. "Fourth pew on the left."

She walked back toward the sanctuary looking back over her shoulder several times as if to make sure Violet was still there.

Violet stared out the glassed window through the dusty darkness and up into the sky. "Oh Lord, I can't bear it if you take one more thing from me. I love him, and if you take Seth, then you'd better be prepared to take me too!"

"Sounds like a threat." Violet jerked back from the door and whirled around. Her eyes traveled up a pair of tan trousers, his blue shirt, and sought Seth's face. He grinned.

"Seth!" She flew into his arms. "Oh, Seth, I was so worried! I thought something happened to you!"

"So I gathered." He held her close.

"Where have you been?" She pounded her fist on his chest. "I tried calling you! I tried your cell, the office, I was going to call your house, but then I didn't have the number."

Seth closed his eyes, absorbing the feel of her in his arms. He looked down at her flushed face. "I am sorry you were worried. I never meant to cause you any grief. I had to go out of town to finalize some papers, and with the roads getting bad, it took longer to get back than I anticipated."

Violet sagged with relief against him. "Why didn't you call me?"

Seth reached down on his hip and showed her his phone. "Battery is dead."

Violet punched him. "Don't ever do that again."

He shied away and held up his hand. "Scout's honor." She grimaced at him and then smiled before slipping her hand in his.

"Where is your jacket?" she asked as they went down the hall towards the sanctuary.

"I had to park on the street, so I came in through the back." Lord, she was beautiful. He knew he would cherish this moment forever. When he walked up behind her and heard her murmur those words, 'I love him' a burst of pure joy hit him squarely in the chest.

Seth opened the doors to the sanctuary and escorted her inside. He led her toward the sanctuary, but she paused on the other side of the doors. He gave her hand a gentle squeeze.

Her eyes looked up at him, large and sad and pleading. "I don't think I can do this," she said. As quietly as they came in, they stepped back out of the sanctuary into the hall.

"The woman who just threatened her wrath on the Lord is afraid to enter His house?"

"The last time I walked through those doors, I was wearing a white velvet gown, but nobody was here for a wedding. Everyone came dressed and prepared for a funeral —except me."

Seth's felt the pressure in his chest, and it ached for the pain that she had borne. "And now you're here again, not for a wedding, or a funeral, but for a celebration of life."

"I felt as if my life had been canceled that day, like my wedding. I sat on the end of the first pew, even when they'd carted the casket away. Outside, the sanctuary life went on, but for me, it stood still. I just sat. Waiting. Nathan came, and I refused to leave. There wasn't a day that I didn't wish Nathan had drowned in Kyle's place."

Seth leaned down, kissing her forehead and caressing her cheek with his thumb.

"When you were late …"

"I'm here now." Seth stroked her cheek.

"And here I am again, standing in the very same place my life started and stopped at the same time, but I don't feel like the same person." She took a shaky breath. "I meant what I said when you walked up. I've got a long road ahead of me where God is concerned, but we're working it out—He and I."

"Violet, this Christmas, next Christmas, and fifty Christmas's from now, I'll be standing right here alongside you, and Kyle will always be here." He touched the place of her heart.

"I know." Deep down, she did. She had loved Kyle, and he'd always be a part of her, but it wasn't the same as this new feeling that grew in her heart for Seth. Her chin trembled, and her lip quivered. "But I can't ever love you like I loved him."

"Love is never the same with other people," Seth said. "We were not intended to love that way."

"How can you be so certain?"

"The same way I'm certain about what's going to happen next."

"What's that?"

"You and I are about to step over the threshold." He held open the door for her. Music flooded the quiet hallway, and his eyes met hers and held them in his gaze. He extended his hand and led her through the doorway.

15

Red bows and shiny wrapped boxes lay beneath the tree in the living room. From inside the kitchen came sounds of rattling pans and voices while Violet sat on the end of her mother's couch, sipping eggnog. Gloria sat, rocking her babe, and humming as she nursed in the far corner. Seth and Nathan stood talking and discussing the different variations of trees and switching now and then to the housing market.

Now that Nathan and Gloria had Christine, they'd eventually move out of Nathan's one-bedroom cabin and into something a little bigger, more equipped for a family.

While he talked, Seth would look over at her and smile. Elaine and Mary Lou Jones shooed her from the kitchen as they cleaned up from dinner.

She watched Nathan bend down and touch the cheek of his nursing babe and smile at his wife. Seth, too, had seen, and his gaze met hers.

He walked over and held out his hand to her. "Why don't we go for a drive?"

"We haven't exchanged gifts yet," Violet said, looking forward to gathering around the tree with her family and Seth.

"We'll wait," Gloria said.

"There's no rush," Nathan said.

"What do you say? There's someplace I'd like to take you." Seth shrugged in the direction of the door.

"Where are we going?"

"You'll see." He pulled her to her feet.

He fetched her coat and wrapped her in the warm wool lining before taking her hand and leading her outside. His brown eyes were like liquid cinnamon that sparkled with anticipation. She, too, felt it building inside her. Giddy with what was to come, she slid into the SUV.

She watched from the frosted window as he drove her out of town. "So, are you going to tell me where we're going? Or do I have to guess?"

"If I tell you, it won't be a surprise, now would it?"

He glanced over at her, flashing a white-tooth grin.

She settled back into the upholstered seat, watching the blur of the town fade away, and the crisp white scenery around them unfold. She gazed out at the frozen lake and glazed ice trees.

"Know where we are?" Seth asked.

Violet glanced over at him. "Shelby Lake?" She looked again out the window.

"I know how much you have a fondness for this place."

"Nathan and Gloria live out by Guist Creek," Violet said.

They pulled up into the driveway of a quaint little house. Violet peered out at the classic arts and crafts type bungalow. Its teal exterior and chunky white columns welcomed her to the flat front porch. She stepped out of the SUV, not waiting for Seth to come around and open her door.

She scanned the snow-blanketed lawn. A large apple tree stood bare by the far side of the house. Her heart swelled at the thought of living here.

"I don't see a for sale sign."

"That's because it's not for sale." He got out and opened

the door for her. "Shall we?"

She stared at him for a moment, skeptical of his motive. "For rent?"

It was bad enough she was planning on moving in with her mother, but bringing her here seemed like torture. Without selling her current residence, she'd had to drop the purchase of her new house.

As he led her up the walk to the front door, she glanced up towards the heavens and prayed. *Help me to understand the reasoning of this in your plan for me.*

"I thought maybe you'd like to see inside." He opened the door and motioned for her to step through the threshold. She prepared herself for a frigid cold house, remembering there had been no heat the last time Seth showed her a home. Yet, this house was warm. Seth helped her as she shrugged off her jacket.

The walls had been freshly painted beige, and the floors polished. Violet walked through the house, every room had been cleaned, painted, and the place had been partially furnished.

Seth stayed back at the entrance, shrugging off his own coat.

"Needs a woman's touch, don't you think?"

"I suppose." She traced her hands across the windowpane cupboards.

"I picked it up on the market a few years ago. The interior house sustained water damage and mold due to a pipe burst and had to be totally redone."

Jolted, Violet stared at him. "This is your house?"

"I use it mainly for clients coming in from out of town, and when I feel like doing a little ice fishing."

"But you live with your grandmother."

"No sense in coming out here and living alone."

Violet's heart jerked. Seth turned and reached over to the countertop for a small velvet box. "Merry Christmas, Violet."

Lost for words, she took the small box from his hands. Her throat tightened as she opened it. As if God's hands wrapped around the earth and held everything, including time, nothing but the beating of her heart rang in her ears. She gulped in deep breaths of air. She closed her eyes and shook her head. When the haze inside her mind finally cleared, she gazed down at a shining silver key inside the box.

"It's the key to this house."

She gazed around the remodeled kitchen, then back at his face. "I can't accept this."

She handed him back the box. Seth took her hand, holding the box, in his. "What if I told you that it was more than the house? What if I said that it's the key to my heart?"

"Does this mean what I think it means?"

"It means that I love you, and I want to marry you. But I'm not going to ask until you're ready."

Her eyes locked on him. A chord of fear uncoiled down her spine as if she were about to relive the past all over again. She couldn't bear to do that, hadn't she prayed and prayed for God to heal her. Deep inside, the old tremors returned. This was *his* house.

She couldn't bear the painful thought of accepting another proposal and attending another funeral. She refused to live in someone else's house. She'd been praying and praying for God to bring her home. Had this been the answer to her prayer?

"Why would you do this?"

"It's my gift to you." He released her hand and set the box down on the counter behind him. "That day, when you sat in my office and sacrificed your home in order to cut your ties with the Freemans, I knew I loved you. I want this to be our home. Your home, so you won't have to move in with Elaine until the time comes that we can be married."

"What about your grandmother and your business?"

"Gram will be just fine on her own, besides I think she and

Elaine have been keeping each other company, and as far as my business goes—you let me worry about that."

"There's no place here for me."

"There's a workshop in the back that you can use to make your beauty products, and we can find you a storefront. I happen to know an excellent realtor."

"But, I have nothing to give you." She'd given everything she had to the Freemans and to her family, and now she stood before Seth with nothing left. She thought about the gift-wrapped under the tree back at her mother's house for him, not even it could compare to the gift he gave her.

"Your love, that's all I'm asking." He took her hand in his. "I can wait until you're ready for everything else."

"I do love you." She watched him hold her hand and, with the other hand, pull the key from its box. As he placed it in her hand, she snatched her fingers back. "I'm sorry. I can't."

Seth's jaw tensed. He grabbed her hand and forced the key into her palm. "Take it, it's yours."

"Seth …"

"We should probably be getting back now." He strolled off into the living room to fetch their jackets. Violet stood inside the kitchen, holding the key.

The drive back to Elaine's house was quiet. Violet sat on the passenger side, staring down at the key in her hand. He forced himself to focus on the road and the path that lay ahead. Where he was going beyond taking her home, he didn't know.

As he pulled up into the driveway, she glanced over at him. He slid from the driver seat and walked around the other side of the SUV. He jerked, opened the door, and held it for her. As she slid out, she looked up at him like a wounded sparrow. He shut the door behind her and walked her to the door.

"You're not coming in?" she asked when he turned to

leave.

He looked back over his shoulder. "I'm not sure that's a good idea."

"Wait! I haven't given you my gift." She turned the knob and went into the house. A few minutes later, she came rushing back out with his gift.

"It's not much …"

Seth took the gift, she'd expect him to open it now, but the thrill of the holiday tradition of exchanging gifts no longer heightened his spirits. "It doesn't have to be. I just appreciate the thought."

He turned and walked away.

"What will you do now?" Tracy stacked the last of the boxes against the wall.

"I don't know." Seth sat in his office, leaning back in a chair. "I've managed to make a few connections from Louisville through the years. I've got an appointment with Jack Daniels later this afternoon."

Tracy leaned against the doorway of his office for the last time. "It's not like you to give up. Besides, we can both look at this slow period as a blessing. Bob won't be so upset all the time about having our family time interrupted, and you can head up to the lake for some ice fishing. As cold as it has been, I'm sure the lake is frozen by now."

"It is. We went skating on the lake before Christmas."

"We? You mean that Harding woman?" Tracy asked.

Seth stared at the unopened gift on his desk.

Tracy angled her head, "You gonna open that?"

Seth turned the box around, tugged gently on the silver ribbon, but not so much as to open it. He felt like that ribbon was the only thing holding him together right now, one tug, and he'd fall apart.

"Some things are best left alone, but if you leave them for too long, it might be too late," she said before heading out.

From inside his desk drawer, he pulled out a paper bag and pulled down the top to reveal the neck of Jack Daniels.

Violet stood in the garage and watched the truck pull away. On the back of the flatbed trailer had been Kyle's car. She'd put the keys in an envelope and mailed them to the attorney as she stepped off the porch for the very last time.

Her room had been left as it always had been. With the patchwork quilt still on her bed, and her mother had turned down the bed. It felt odd coming back home, but wasn't that what she had wanted?

She could hear her mother downstairs bustling about. They, her mother and Nathan, had spent the morning helping her pack up her things and move in with her mother again. She tossed her suitcase on the bed.

Nathan's room was across the hall, now filled with boxes of her belongings, and her mother had made room for the few items of furniture she'd brought with her. At least she still had her bed, pressing her hand down on the patchwork quilt.

She opened her suitcase and took out the Bible lying on top. She placed it on the desk under her window, where'd she'd be sure to find it in the morning. Beside it, she set the shining silver house key.

She'd spent many a night since Seth's proposal reading her Bible, and in the wee hours of the morning, she'd prayed for Seth.

She found her mother downstairs in the kitchen preparing supper.

"There are plenty of leftovers, and I thought we'd have lemon pie for dessert," Elaine said, as Violet entered the kitchen.

"Sounds great." She walked over to the refrigerator and helped pull out dishes.

"I'm so glad you decided to come home." Elaine got all teary-eyed and shooed away the tears with her hand as she turned away to the sink.

Violet didn't know what to say, she forced a smile and spooned cold mashed potatoes onto a plate. This was her first night home, and yet she didn't feel as if she'd come home at all.

Her thoughts were always on Seth.

"This week, the girls will be coming over for our weekly Bible study, and you can join us. I already told Mary Lou to grab an extra book for you this Wednesday." Elaine chattered on as she popped ham in the microwave, and Violet stood spooning another lump of mash potatoes on her plate.

"My, you must be hungry. It will be nice cooking for someone else again for a change."

Violet paused and looked down at her plate; she had enough mashed potatoes to feed an army. She picked up the plate and scraped them all back.

"Aren't you going to eat now?"

She didn't have the heart to tell her mother she'd lost her appetite. But when Elaine pulled out the lemon pie, Violet couldn't resist the temptation of dessert.

"Maybe just a slice of pie."

"You have to eat something ..."

"Mother ..."

Elaine placed her hands on either side of Violet's face, "Oh, Violet, it's so good to hear you say that again."

Violet sighed; maybe coming home wasn't what she needed. In her heart, home was no longer a place as much as it was a person. She climbed back up the stairs to her room, curled up on her bed, and clutched her Bible along with Seth's key.

16

"He's not here."

Violet turned from inside Seth's office. Tracy heaved a large box on top of her desk and filled it with files.

"Do you know when he'll be back?" Violet asked.

"He didn't say." Tracy opened the drawers of her desk.

Violet felt her brows furrow together. "Would you mind giving him a message?"

Tracy turned from her task and looked Violet square in the eye. "Do I look like his secretary?"

"No, but you're his partner, right?"

"And I'm his friend, which is more than I can say about someone else right now." Tracy pulled out several files and laid them on her desk.

"I suppose I had that coming. It's just that ..."

Tracy held up her hand. "Forgive me. It's not my business. Things around here are ... well ..."

"I had no idea it was this bad," Violet said.

"Honey, you don't know the half of it." Tracy snapped her fingers and walked around the desk towards Violet. "I found this in his office after he left." She pulled out an empty bottle of Jack Daniels from the trash.

Violet stared at her. What did an empty bottle of alcohol have to do with Seth? Surely, it wasn't his. It could belong to anyone. Couldn't it?

"Eight years." Tracy shook her head and shoved the bottle in Violet's hands. "Then you come along, enough to tempt a man to drink again. Lord knows he's a strong one, but we've all got our weaknesses. I guess he couldn't find anyone else to lean on."

Violet gazed down at the bottle. The foul smell wafted up from inside the container. Dread flowed through her veins and seeped into her soul.

"Do you have any idea where he'd be?"

Tracy shrugged, "Hard to say, Sportsmen's Club isn't too far from here, I think he mentioned something about it the other day."

Violet winced. She remembered the first day she'd met him, and she'd told him where to find the Sportsmen's Club. She'd been horrible to him then, too.

"Where are you going?" Tracy asked.

Violet set the bottle on the desk and trotted past her. "The Sportsmen's Club to find Seth."

Tracy reached out and grabbed her by the arm. "Wait, you'll need this if you want to get in that place today." Tracy reached into the box, shuffled through some papers, and handed Violet an invitation. "Good luck."

Outside the Sportsmen's Club, Violet spotted Seth's SUV in the parking lot. She opened the invitation and found a ticket for admittance to a fashion show. Violet grabbed her purse and entered the establishment.

A line had formed at the bar, but she didn't spot Seth there, nor at any of the tables where mostly ladies sat sampling appetizers. A large runway made of covered tables divided the open room.

"Ticket, dear?" an elderly woman asked from the entrance. Violet put on her most polite smile and handed her ticket to the woman. "You're at table four. I'm told there's a handsome young gentleman at that table." She winked. "Not many of those here."

Violet patted the woman on the arm. "No, there's not very many."

She walked around, and out of the corner of her eye, she saw him. On his arm clung another woman, and her heart sank. He wore his sweater tied around his shoulders like a pro golf jock, and his sunglasses were pushed up into the thick curls of his hair. The woman beside him smiled, and as if he told a joke, she laughed.

Obviously, Seth wasn't in any danger here. She turned around to leave when she bumped into Mary Lou Jones. Mary Lou gasped as her glass spilled onto her blouse. "Violet!"

"Oh, I'm so sorry. I didn't mean to run into you." Violet searched for a napkin or a towel for Mary Lou.

"Oh, don't worry about it. It's just water." Mary Lou said, plucking the material of her shirt from her shoulder. "Are you here to sell your beauty products?"

"No."

"Oh, what a shame, I'm sure you could have made out very well today." Mary Lou pointed over at a table where Anne Patterson's mother Barbara sat along with Megan Markle, a friend of Elaine's. "Won't you sit down and join me. I think they are going to start soon."

Violent glanced around the table to the one empty seat. She wondered if her mother was here, too. The last thing she wanted to do was encounter Elaine and have to explain this to her mother. "I have to go. I just was stopping in to see …"

"Seth," Mary Lou took hold of Violet's arm. "Why don't you come sit?"

Violet looked between Seth and the door and then gave in to Mary Lou's request. The other women smiled and murmured their greetings before carrying on their conversation without her. She ignored the glances and the polite smiles.

They knew. Gossip ran rapid in Hidden Hills. This was a mistake, but as she went to get back up, Mary Lou laid a hand on her arm. "It was a very strong thing that you did. Seth told me you rejected his proposal."

As Violet opened her mouth to protest, Mary Lou held up her hand. "Nobody is judging you, dear. I believe that each person must find their own way through the brambles that come across the paths of which we walk in the Lord's favor. You've had more than you're share. Just like Seth."

Violet settled down in her chair and stared out across the sea of guests at him. When he lifted his head and his eyes met hers, she felt her stomach quiver.

Mary Lou leaned closer to her to keep their conversation more private. "He lost someone very dear to him, too. Although my Beth is still alive, I pray each night that she'll come back one day."

"Beth is Seth's Mother?"

"Lost soul, my Beth, still wandering through the world trying to find her way, unwilling to accept a hand for strength. That's why she brought me her only son to raise and give him the one thing she couldn't."

Violet's neck burned and her cheeks felt flush, Seth tore his gaze away from her, and Violet turned back to Mary Lou. "What's that?"

Mary Lou took a sip of her drink and laid her frail hand upon Violet's. "Love."

Violet blinked, unsure if she'd heard the older woman correctly. "Love?"

"My Donald and I tried as we did; Beth wasn't one to share herself with anyone. Not even her son, but I think she realized that a baby needed more than milk and diapers. After Seth's father left her, she couldn't bring herself to find joy in the blessing of God's love, or accept the responsibility of giving love in return." Mary Lou sighed, "Seth's a good man, he's got a good heart, and until he told me about you,

Violet, I was beginning to think he'd shut himself off, like my Beth."

Violet sat back in her chair, absorbing this new bit of information about Seth. A woman stepped up on the makeshift stage, her face familiar, but Violet couldn't remember the name. Sonya? Maybe? After a short welcome, the fashion show started. She wasn't late, after all.

It turned out that all the ladies were single mothers and this was a fundraiser to help finance their way back through school. Seth, along with the town's local handyman Sam Brink, escorted the models back and forth from the stage.

She had no doubt now that Tracy had led her here on false pretenses, but the fact of the empty bottle still tugged at her consciousness.

As water wears away stones and torrents wash away the soil, so you destroy man's hope ... She recalled the words from a passage she'd read in her Bible. She mustered up every ounce of a smile toward Mary Lou and the others as she politely excused herself.

She shouldn't have come here; she had no place amongst these people, and no right to approach Seth. She slipped around the tables and headed for the door.

Outside she welcomed the sharp intake of cold air into her lungs, every breath she drew ached into her ribs, but she supposed she deserved it.

Behind her she heard the metal doors open. "Still running, I see." His voice was harsh, and she could detect a hint of annoyance. "Can't seem to ever stay in one place, can you?"

She deserved that, coming from Seth. She turned to face him. "I came to see you, but you're obviously busy. I'll catch up with you another time."

He stood with his legs apart, and his breath steamy from the cold. His fist clenched at his sides.

She hadn't come to fight with him. She'd never seen him like this. His eyes, always so compassionate and kind, looked down at her with belligerence. One she recognized as doing herself many times to cover the pain.

"Why not now? You did say you came to see me, right?" He crossed his arms in front of his chest.

"I was worried about you." The chill of this January afternoon nipped at her nose and kissed her cheeks as she spoke. "I stopped by your office ..."

"Things are slow, so I decided to take a few days off."

"So I gathered," she said, as briskly as the wind. "Tracy told me you'd be here. I brought you this." She dug into her handbag and held out an envelope to him, much like the one Tracy had given her.

Seth laughed,. "I don't want any more of your gifts."

Violet sniffed, lowered her hand, and grimaced. "I guess I deserve that. If you'll just take this, I'll explain everything."

She saw it then, the flicker in his eyes, and she held her breath. She offered him the envelope once more. "I love you, but there is just one more thing I have to do before I could ever commit to marrying you."

Seth's eyebrows shot up. "Is that what you think? That you have to marry me to live in the house? There's no strings attached, marry me or not, the house is yours to live in."

"It's just that you offered me a house, and you said you would wait and ..." Violet felt the cold seep through the barrier of her jacket. "I have to do this, and I would appreciate it if you would be there to support me when I do."

"I never offered you happy ever after," he said. "It's not mine to promise. Only God knows the time we have here on earth. Though He may not be the one to push us into the dark valleys, He is the one who would be our guiding light and see us out of them."

She regretted it before she said it, but the words slipped out before she could halt them. "Did God show you the light before or after you sought him at the bottom of a bottle?"

Seth stomped his feet. "Why don't we go inside where it's warm and talk?"

Violet sensed the change in him, he was offering her an olive branch, and she grasped hold of it. She followed him back inside. He led her to a bench beneath a rack of coats, and she sat beside him. Just the slight contact of their hips brushing caused warmth to creep back into her cold veins.

"I take it you found the empty bottle in my office." He rubbed his hands together. "I never drank that bottle."

"Then why was it there?"

"I've always kept temptation one drawer pull away from me since the day I stopped letting it control me."

She placed her hands in his, rubbing his long, lean fingers with her own to circulate the warmth in his hands again.

"I'm an alcoholic, Violet." His eyes searched to see if she'd cast judgment, and when he found none, he went on. "I joined Alcoholics' Anonymous almost six years ago. I was drowning in life, drowning in work, and then one day, my mother showed up. I was in pretty bad shape, could hardly stand up for an open house, and here she comes waltzing in looking like a bloody Mary, all dressed up in a red suit and her holier than thou attitude. "

"I'd always pictured the day my mother would come back. I was twenty-four years old, it was my first open house, and she gave me a tongue lashing I'll never forget. I wasn't her child, I wasn't worthy of her love, and I'd never be in the condition she'd found me."

"How do you know this woman was your mother?" Violet asked.

"She introduced herself, she used her maiden name, admitted she'd never married my father, and that she had no place for mistakes in her life."

Violet squeezed his hands tighter. "There are no mistakes in God's design where human life is concerned."

Seth leaned forward and kissed her cheek. "That's along

the same lines my grandmother said. I could see in my grandmother's eyes the pain I'd caused her, and so that night, I
gathered every bottle from my hiding places, and instead of
going to an establishment where I'd visit often, I found myself
at an AA meeting. The first thing they teach you is to take it
one day at a time. And every day, I'd want to hold that bottle,
taste it, smell it, and every time I was tempted, I'd hear my
mother's voice and pray for the strength to make it one more
day."

"The bottle in your drawer?" Violet asked.

"It has been there ever since. At first, I told myself it was
there if I needed a drink. I've taken it out a few times, held it,
and then put it back. Each time, I'd find something to distract
me from taking another drink. Just like that last night in my
office, when I pulled it out, only it was your gift that kept me
from taking a drink."

"The gift I gave you for Christmas?" Violet wasn't sure
how to react. "It was just an ornament."

"It was more than that." He brushed the knuckles of his
hand across her cheek. "It was Christmas when my mother
left me with my Grandmother when I was little. That year, my
grandmother helped me, and I made a special ornament that
I hang on the tree every year, just for her. I say a little prayer,
hang it on the tree, and have faith that my mother will be in
good health all year and that she may decide to come home
again.

"When I opened your gift and pulled out the handmade
ornament, it reminded me of that faith, hope, and love. It was
as if there had already been a prayer said for me, and that
ornament had become the messenger.

"I poured the contents of the bottle down the drain and
tossed the bottle into my trash can."

"What a relief." Violet gushed. "I was so afraid I'd driven
you to that bottle."

Seth laughed, "I admit, you're not the easiest woman to

fall in love with, but not enough to drive a man to drink. Although, I'll admit a few times it came close." She could tell by his light tone that he teased her, and it made her smile.

"I don't want to hold you any longer, I'm sure you need to be getting back," Violet said, relieved and overjoyed that Seth hadn't fallen from his faith or broken his sobriety. "I've never been one to depend on others, and I may not be ready to be your wife yet, but if you could come with me next Saturday night, it would mean a lot to me."

Seth took the envelope she offered him. "I wouldn't miss it for the world."

17

Every stitch of clothing she owned was tossed across the top of her bed. This was foolish. She and Seth had been out countless times, but not like this. Fast food restaurants and take out didn't count. Tonight, they were going somewhere extra special. There would be dinner. She'd sit down with people she didn't know, yet their reasons for being there would be similar to her own.

She'd made sure to invite the Freemans. She didn't want them to miss the main feature of tonight's charity auction. The local news would be covering the event. Kyle Freeman's first race car had not only been on display during the auto show, but tonight, it would be sold to the highest bidder. Predictions across the state were estimated at just over a million. Bidding had gone live on eBay that morning. Already phone calls filled her mother's answering machine. Several talk shows had offered her a spot. Everyone wanted an interview.

Violet planted her hands on her hips, scanning what was left in her closet. Tonight, she needed something more than her casual attire. She picked up a pair of black silk pants and a glittering V-necked blouse.

Checking her appearance in the bathroom mirror, she frowned. She looked like a widow. She watched the outfit crumble to the floor when she caught a glimpse of purple and pulled it from beneath the pile on her bed. Perfect.

Violet was putting the last smear of gloss to her lips when the doorbell rang. She smoothed down the wrinkles in the front of her gown and headed downstairs feeling giddy, like a schoolgirl on her first date, and her mother smiled at her from another room.

She opened the door. Seth's face was blocked by a dozen white roses.

"They're beautiful." She stepped back as he handed her the bouquet. Violet turned, determined to put them in water before they left when her mother came into the room.

"I'll take those. My, they are beautiful." Elaine buried her face in the scent of the buds.

"Are you sure you won't join us?" Violet asked.

"The girls will be coming over tonight. We're on the last chapter of this study, besides you don't need your mother tagging along on a night like this." Elaine waved her hand at them. "Now, go on and have a nice evening."

Violet smiled, reached over and hugged her mother. "Thank you for understanding."

As Elaine walked away, Seth reached out and touched a strand of Violet's hair. "Have I told you how beautiful you look?"

"No, you haven't."

"Gorgeous. Absolutely gorgeous."

She felt the color rise in her cheeks.

The deep purple satin gown wrapped up around her neck, sculpting and molding her natural curves.

She reached by the door for a wool jacket, and Seth held it while she slipped her arms inside. As they left the house, Violet noticed one of the living room curtains pulled pack, and her mother spying out the window.

Violet laid her head back against the seat. Seth closed the door coming around to the driver's side. "You're not going to fall asleep on me, are you?" he chided, buckling his seatbelt.

Her nerves tingled, and her stomach quivered. "Not a chance."

Soft wisps of hair curled fashionably around her face. She pulled one back and swirled it back into the bun at the nape of her neck. Two long black chopsticks with rhinestones held it in place.

It didn't take long for the press and all those in attendance to discover who she was, once they took their seats at the governor's table. Several times the press had pestered her, and each time she gave them the same comment. "Kyle was a free spirit. His faith, like his racing, was focused and unyielding. He always considered himself the underdog, and that's why I know he'd want the proceeds to go to the missionary efforts to help those affected by the recent earthquakes in Haiti."

"His family doesn't seem to have the same opinion," Seth said. The press fed between her and the family, only she wasn't angry and protesting like the Freemans. Miranda Freeman stood in front of the cameras woefully teary-eyed and clutching her younger son by the arm while her husband verbalized his protest of the sale.

Dinner was served, and the crowds settled down. Violet was glad Kyle would never witness his family's behavior. She leaned towards Seth, whispered in his ear, and together they bowed their heads to pray for the Freeman family.

When the main course arrived, Violet's eyes focused on her plate. Seth kept an arm slung over the back of her chair, listening to their table host discuss the recent tragedies due to natural disasters over the years.

Dessert arrived, and Violet found her stomach entwined in small knots. She rested a hand on her clutch bag, where inside, she'd placed Seth's key. A slow sensation of relief sated her for a time, and she sat back to take a bite of her dessert.

"Ladies and gentlemen," a dark-haired woman sang sweetly into the podium's microphone from the front of the room. "I'd like to first welcome you to this momentous occasion. Each year, we pull in new models of cars here at the auto show, introduce new technologies, and continue to address safety issues."

"Car manufacturers are able to predict, test, and accommodate for possible accidents. That's why each year, new models of vehicles are being designed for safety, economy, and protecting the environment we live in. However, the natural disasters that plague our world, like the recent earthquakes in Latin America, are unpredictable and can't be tested."

"Kyle Freeman was just as unpredictable as an earthquake or any other natural disaster, no one knew what to expect from this rookie race car driver, who within the first two years of his career won the NASCAR Championship Cup."

A picture of Kyle holding up his cup and leaning against the car flashed across several projector screens. Violet felt a tear trickle down her cheek. She reached over and took Seth's hand for reassurance.

From somewhere in the back, she heard the unmistakable wails of a mother scorned. Television cameras rolled, focused on the speaker for the entire nation to view live.

"Two years ago, as a nation, we mourned the loss of this great race car driver. Tonight, we are honored to have been able to display the car that Kyle Freeman won his first NASCAR championship in. Gifted to his fiancée, Violet Harding, she has generously donated it to the disaster relief efforts of the missionaries in Haiti. So, with no further delay, we will now turn the bidding over to our auctioneer as the final minutes are approaching."

Oh Lord, please use Kyle's car to do good, that the money would be of assistance to those who are in need, and that the lost may be found just as you found me, blinded by despair.

Seth squeezed her hand. A gentleman's voice rambled numbers as spotlights shone in the darkness, and Kyle's car was illuminated behind the auctioneer.

"Are you alright?" Seth's voice was tender. "We don't have to stay until the end if you don't want."

"No," She looked at him, found herself wanting, and placed a hand on his cheek. Around them, the room seemed to fade away, and the auctioneer's voice was a mere buzz in her ears.

"I'm ready now," she said, searching his eyes that she may know his heart.

He took her hand from his face and held it inside his. "Are you sure?"

"Ask me." Violet's heart skipped a beat.

The auctioneer had smacked his gavel, and Kyle's car was sold.

Violet stood out on the dock behind Nathan and Gloria's cabin near Shelby Lake.

Before her, the ice stretched out for miles. She stuck her gloved hands in her coat pockets. It was warm for February, but the cold kissed her cheeks, and the wind made her shiver. She didn't turn her head when she heard someone behind her. Gloria was nursing the baby, and Nathan offered to join her outside once he finished the dishes.

"I hear the sunset is spectacular from here."

Violet turned to find Seth strolling down the dock. "It reflects on the lake. There's nothing more beautiful."

"I can think of one thing." Seth slipped his arms around her. He leaned close and said, "You." He lowered his mouth to hers.

Violet felt the dock beneath her sway. He slipped his

fingers into her hair, and her coat hood fell back, sending small shivers down her scalp, her neck, and her spine. He deepened their kiss, and she pulled him closer. She had wondered how long it would take before he kissed her like this.

He'd kissed her the night after he took her home from the auto show in Lexington. The passion in his eyes, his tenderness, she hadn't wanted him to stop.

She could go on kissing him all evening, tucked warm into his embrace, and miss the sunset. Seth pulled away, grinning from ear to ear.

"How did the house showing go?" She nestled closer into his arms.

"I think they liked it. I look for them to come back for a second showing in a few days."

"You missed it. Nathan caught a perch today. I'm surprised you didn't go ice fishing with him this morning."

"I didn't think the ice was thick enough. Even though we're in February now, it's been getting warmer instead of colder. I don't plan on breaking any ice diving records this season."

Violet shivered.

"If you're cold, we can go inside," he said.

She glanced toward the cabin. Nathan was watching from his kitchen window. "Not yet. I was hoping to watch the sunset."

"I'd hoped you would say that." He pressed his warm cheek against her. "I've been meaning to ask you something."

Violet's heart went aflutter. She didn't want to hope. She didn't want anything to ruin this blissful moment as raspberry tinted clouds, and orange rays spread overhead. Beyond the lake, a dark burning globe of gold glistened against the snow-covered ground.

There was no one else she wanted to share this moment with more than Seth. It was if God knew what was in her heart, and he'd sent Seth here to be with her for just this moment.

"Ask me." It wasn't so much a command, but a plea. She felt for the key in her pocket and held it out to him. "I've been holding onto this. It's more than the key to your lake house, you told me it was the key to your heart, and I want to unlock it."

"You have." He placed his hand over the key and tugged her back to him. His lips came crashing down, distracting her from any second thoughts. Wholeheartedly, she returned his kiss before stepping back. She wasn't about to let him kiss his way out of it this time.

Around her heart, a new shield formed. She stiffened in his arms. "I can't hold onto another man's house, not without …"

"Being his wife?" Seth finished for her.

She saw it then in his eyes, the way they sparkled with joy and mirth. He tightened his hold on her hand around the key. "I want that, too."

There on the snow-laden deck with the sun illuminating the lake with glittery sparkles of gold and raspberry hues, Seth bent on one knee. Violet's chest tightened. She gripped his hand, but he gently slid his away. He took her hand in both of his, removing first the key, then finger by finger he took off her glove. He rubbed her flesh to keep her palm from growing cold.

"I hope you don't mind. It's something old. A tradition of sorts. It belonged to my grandfather's mother. It passed to my grandmother when they were engaged, and I had it fitted for you." Seth pulled a gold and silver entwined ring from inside his coat. There was a small chip of stone in a cluster of other stones.

"I would be honored," Violet said, and she meant it.

"Then you will marry me?"

Violet laughed. She stared down at this man who made

her heart warm. She found love inside her for him; she didn't dare hope would conceive after her grief. "I thought you'd never ask."

Seth slid the ring on her barren finger and kissed it before he stood. Suddenly, the sunset couldn't hold in comparison to the joy residing in her heart.

EPILOGUE

Violet sipped her flute of sparkling white grape juice. Spring had turned her backyard into a variety of colors. Bright-blossom flowers, shades of green, and gentle hues of lavender floated gracefully from limb to lawn. Seating lined the full dock at Shelby Lake.

Guests gathered near the lake, listening to the church choir sing from the dock. Round tables with lawn chairs scattered across the space of the backyard. Their entire church family had come to gather on this day to celebrate their union.

A soft laugh escaped Violet's lips watching Nathan's face scowl at his infant daughter. Gloria reached up with a cloth, too late to save his tuxedo jacket from spilled milk.

Gloria looked radiant in the lavender gown she wore. A few days before, Violet had been pleased with the new shorter hairstyle Gloria had chosen. It exposed her face and opened her smile. A touch of ripe red lipstick and beige on her eyes had transformed the new mother's tired face into a glowing beauty.

Violet folded her arm onto the other and held up the flute in her hand to take a sip. Perhaps if it were God's will, in a year or two, she too would know the blessings of motherhood.

The wind blew, billowing her veil out behind her. Her eyes scanned through the guests. She giggled. Anne and Pete's youngest son reached up and poked a finger in her wedding cake. His fingers covered in icing, he looked around, stuffing his fingers in his mouth.

Violet could no longer hold them in. She erupted in giggles.

"What's so funny?" Seth's voice brushed against her ear. He came from behind, wrapping his arms around her waist.

Violet glanced back at him. "I think we should cut the cake." She turned in his arms to face him.

"Hungry, Mrs. Jones?" His lips curved upward.

"No," She traced the line of his jaw with her fingertip. "But I'd say one of our guests is." She jerked her chin toward the cake. "He's already sampled the frosting."

Seth chuckled, glancing over at the table where the cake sat. They watched as the little boy licked his short stubby fingers one by one.

"Not for long." Anne came around the table grabbing the child by the elbow. She leaned over, pointing a finger and scolding the boy. Seth and Violet laughed. He hugged her closer to him. "Someday, that'll be you." He kissed the tip of her nose.

"Shall we cut the cake?" Violet asked, sure if they did, the boy would be first in line for a piece.

"In a moment. I just want to hold you."

Violet lightly pushed against him. "You can do that later. I'm afraid if we don't cut our cake now, there won't be any for the rest of our guests to sample."

Seth nuzzled her neck, sweet scents of lavender and berries filled his nostrils. He would never be able to get enough of all the different scents she wore. The faint tinge of vanilla tickled his nose from the candles she had lit around the house before the ceremony. Their house.

Taking her by the hand, he led her toward the cake. Three

layers of lemon frosting greeted them. Each layer carefully sculpted like lace doilies. Pure white daisies with yellow button centers ringed the sides of each layer. At the top sat the bride and groom made of sparkling crystal.

The photographer hurried over and the guests gathered around them. His hand over her hand, they picked up the ivory-handled knife and sliced into the middle layer of cake. Slowly they pulled out the small wedge, placing it on a napkin, and each took a piece in their hand.

Violet's eyes twinkled as she smiled at him. Seth drew his own suspicions and grinned back. On the count of three, they both parted their lips and took a bite of cake. Violet licked her lips, and as Seth bit into the other half of his piece of cake— Violet smashed it into his face.

He glared at her, cake smeared over his cheeks, and up his nose, he was sure. Those around them found humor in his situation and laughed, but Violet backed away from him slowly. Seth's brow arched.

He stalked towards her.

Her expression turned to shock.

"You wouldn't" She took another step back. Seth held a piece of cake poised in his hand, mid-air.

Her eyes grew wide, and she turned to flee through the guests. The crowd parted. Violet picked up the folds of her gown. Two strides and he grabbed her by the arm. "No," she cried, laughing and shielding her face away from him.

Seth caught a glimpse of his grandmother, and Elaine resuming the task of cutting slices from the cake. He looked back at his bride, "Look at me."

He waited for her laughter to subside and turn her face toward him. He wiped the smudge of frosting from the corner of her lips, and as she did, he dipped her low and kissed her.

Clinging to him, she said, "I love you."

"Just remember that twenty years from now, that you're

stuck with me." He pulled her up and licked the frosting from his fingers.

"So now that you have me," She grinned, eyes sparkling, "What is it you plan on doing with me?"

"Loving you." He swept her up into his arms. "For the rest of my days."

He marched her around the front of their lakeside cottage, and she reached for the door handle. As the door swung open, he said "Welcome home."

WHAT'S NEXT?

All Caroline wants is to sort out her messy life while Sam keeps interfering with her Christmas plans.

The girl voted most likely to succeed in high school has nothing to show except a failed marriage and nonexistent career. Plans for a fresh start didn't involve partnering with Caroline's old high school crush to keep her Aunt Marge's floral shop running.

A single dad, Sam works at the Christmas tree farm, doing odd jobs and caring for his son. Sam will do anything to help a friend, but this time he might be too over his head to see the mistletoe.

The holidays are the perfect time for two hearts to unite.

Read **HOLIDAY HEARTS** next.

ABOUT THE AUTHOR

Growing up on a farm in Pennsylvania, Susan Lower yearned for adventure. A woodsy gal, Susan prefers camping over going to the beach any day. Still a farm girl at heart, Susan writes fast action reads filled with cowboys, heroes, and hope. She writes both western historical and contemporary romances, romantic suspense, and has been itching to one day write a mystery or thriller. Christmas is her favorite holiday, and she loves to write resilient characters struggling to overcome the complications of life while holding their values and strengthening their faith.

ALSO BY SUSAN LOWER

Silver Wind Horse Rescue

Forgotten Reins

Unbridled

Silver Stirrups

Hearts of Hidden Hills

Salvaged Hearts

Reckless Hearts

Healing Hearts

Holiday Hearts

Thunder Valley MC

Haden

Rosco

Sebastian

Cowgirl Mysteries

The Cowgirl Gets The Bad Guy

The Cowgirl Takes The Bounty

The Cowgirl Chases The Robbers

Stand Alone

Trade Secrets